Finding Mr. Right

New Adult Sweet Romance Series, Volume 4

Ellie J. Adams

Published by Wheelhouse Publishers LLC, 2018.

Copyright

A Wheelhouse Publishers paperback edition.

Wheelhouse Publishers, LLC

c/o Registered Agents, Inc.

82 Wendell Avenue, Suite 100

Pittsfield, MA 01201

To learn more about Wheelhouse Publishers, visit: wheelhousepublishers.com

CHAPTER 1

Justin Renaud sat at his desk flipping paperclips into a cup. He was bored out of his mind. He hated his job. When he graduated with a degree in business he thought he would do more with it than calculate numbers on a spreadsheet all day.

"Renaud, you have those reports for me yet?!" yelled Chris Roberts, Justin's boss, as he made his way toward Justin's cubicle. The only thing worse than the job was working for Chris. His boss was in his early sixties and stuck in a middle manager position he didn't like.

Is that my future? thought Justin.

"I just emailed them to you," said Justin once Chris reached his cubicle.

"Did you double check the formulas?" asked Chris.

"Yep. We're good to go," replied Justin with a deadpan tone.

"It looks like we aren't giving you enough to do," said Chris as he looked at the pile of paperclips near Justin and those in the half filled cup.

"Can I help it if I'm a wunderkind?" Justin flashed a fake smile.

"You can help with the attitude. I get the distinct impression you don't like working here."

"You are very perceptive, Chris."

"Well, there are lots of guys who'd love to have your job."

"Then why don't you give it to one of them? I quit," said Justin as he stood up and walked past Chris.

"Wait just a second," called Chris. "You think you can just up and leave like that? Well, you can forget a recommendation."

Justin had removed his tie before he reached the end of the hallway. He hated wearing ties. They felt too restrictive. It was a symbol of his job. A job he just quit.

Justin stepped out front of the building of his former employer and pulled his cellphone out of his pocket. He called his oldest brother Andrew. A call that was long overdue.

"Justin," answered Andrew. "What's up little bro?"

"I want to talk to you about opening the restaurant. I just quit my job."

"You what? Justin, was that the best move?"

"I've got money saved up. I'll be okay for a while. I just couldn't take it anymore. I'm not a nine to five kind of guy. If I had to spend another day in that office, I was going to throw myself out the window."

"I get you didn't like the job, but you know how Dave and Matt feel about the property. We haven't all been able to agree on this."

"All the more reason for me to quit. Now they will see I am serious about the restaurant. I can devote myself full time to it."

"Alright. I'll call them, but I can't make any promises. Let's all have dinner tonight and talk about it."

David and Matthew were Justin's other brothers. The four of them had discussed turning the old family restaurant into a newer, more sophisticated, restaurant. One that would appeal to a younger, professional crowd. Well, Justin had discussed it. Andrew supported his idea. David and Matthew did not.

It had been several months since they closed the family restaurant. Their dad no longer wanted to run it. Just another thing he gave up on when it came to the family.

He walked out on them six years ago. That, actually, was a blessing. All Justin could remember of his parents marriage was how much they argued. Constantly. He wondered if they had ever been happy together. The divorce had been ugly.

In the end, Justin's mom ended up with a fifty percent stake in *Renaud's French Cuisine*. Their dad continued to run it until about a year ago. That's when he announced he was closing the restaurant. He handed over his half of the deed to his sons. Each owned an equal share.

Their mom told them to do whatever they wanted with the property. She had no interest in keeping the restaurant open or dealing with what became of the property. It was a prime piece of Manhattan real estate. Justin and Andrew wanted to open a new, hipper, restaurant. David and Matthew wanted to sell the property.

They had spent the better part of the previous six months trying to make a decision. They remained at an impasse. But they all knew that they needed to do something with the property. It was too valuable to just leave sitting empty.

The Renaud brothers gathered around Andrew's dining room table. Andrew was thirty-four, David thirty, Matthew twenty-nine, and Justin twenty-four. You could tell just by looking at them they were brothers. Similar heights, builds, and faces. Andrew was an attorney, David a financial planner, and Matthew a hotel manager.

"Justin, you need to let go of this idea for a new restaurant. The property is worth a fortune. We need to sell it and move on," said David.

"And a successful restaurant could earn us profits for years to come," replied Justin.

"If it's profitable," interjected Matthew.

"So are you saying I would run it into the ground?"

"No one's saying that," said David. "Matthew and I just don't see it as the best use for the property."

"Drew, help me out here," said Justin to Andrew.

"I think we should let Justin have a crack at this. Look, the three of us don't need the money from the sale of the property. Justin needs something to do with his life. More than that, it's what he wants to do with his life," said Andrew.

"This is the same conversation we always have. Dude, you're not offering anything new," said David.

"I quit my job today. I want to devote myself full time to opening a restaurant," replied Justin.

"You what?! You quit your job? Are you insane?" commented Matthew.

"It was killing me. I hated it," answered Justin.

"Just like dad. A quitter," muttered David.

Justin leaped up and reached across the table. "Take that back! I'm nothing like dad!"

"Sit down before I kick your butt," said David.

"Better bring some help," said Justin.

"Cool it! Both of you!" Andrew said as he sat Justin back down. Justin shrugged Andrew off as he took his seat.

"We can't keep having this conversation. Look what it is doing to us," offered Matthew.

"You're right," said Andrew. "So let's make a decision. You know I'm already in favor of Justin opening a new restaurant. You and David have never been keen on the idea. Why don't we do this . . . we all go in as equal co-owners of the restaurant. We each have skills that are an asset. I can handle the legal paperwork; Dave, you can handle the finances; Matt you can help with hospitality. Justin is a natural people person and is as smart, if not smarter, than any of us. I am confident he can effectively manage the restaurant. If we can't turn a profit in a reasonable amount of time, we shut it down and sell. The property will only go up in value. I don't see much downside."

That was the best effort that Andrew had ever made to convince David and Matthew to back Justin's idea to open a new family restaurant. Justin and Andrew looked at each other and then over at David and Matthew. They all sat in silence for a few minutes. David sat back in his chair and let out a sigh.

"If Matt agrees, I'll go along with it. But you only get my vote if Matt is full in on this. Justin, despite what you think, I believe in you. But Matt has solid experience in dealing with customers. I want to know he will be available to guide you."

"Okay," said Matthew. "But I'm not going to loose my shirt over this. None of us should. We'll need to get the financing for this from the bank."

"We can use the property as collateral," said Justin. "It's worth more than what we'll need for start-up costs. If we had to, not that we will, we could sell and pay the bank back."

"So we're all agreed, then?" asked Andrew.

"Yes," said Matthew.

"Yes," concurred David.

"Well, it looks like the Renaud boys are going to own a new family restaurant," Andrew said.

"Don't screw this up," David said to Justin.

"Get lost," replied Justin with a smile.

David smiled back. Justin was smart and great with people. He also seemed to be charmed. David actually had little doubt Justin would make the restaurant a huge success.

"What will we call this restaurant?" asked Matthew.

"*Renaud's*," replied Justin. "It will help bring in some of Dad's former customers as well as signal a new and fresh restaurant. Plus, simply using our name offers the sophistication I am going for."

Their French heritage was strong. They all spoke the language fluently. The brothers all smiled and nodded. *Renaud's*. Perfect.

CHAPTER 2

I had just returned to New York City from a long weekend in Boston. I had been helping my former roommate find a place to live after she accepted a new job there. Kelly and I had been classmates at New York University and rented an apartment together after graduation. I grew up in Newton, Massachusetts so I offered to show Kelly around Boston.

My trip also gave me an opportunity to visit my family. My parents still lived in the same house I grew up in. I have many happy memories of living there. I had a middle class upbringing in a loving and supportive family.

I'm the oldest of three children. My younger sister, by two years, was away at college. My younger brother just started his sophomore year in high school. He was now officially taller than me. I was bummed about that and he didn't let an opportunity go by to remind me he was five feet eight inches tall to my five feet six inches.

Each of us have brown hair. The similarities end there. My brother is now the tallest. He is also pretty muscular and very athletic. He has handsome blue eyes. My sister is five feet five inches, perfectly proportioned, has brown eyes, but is uncoordinated. I'm slender but more toned than my sister. I'm not as athletic as my brother but faster. I'm a runner.

Most would consider us a good-looking family. My brother always has girls trying to go out with him. My sister is stunning. If she were taller, she could be a model. I guess I would consider myself pretty. Not stunning like my sister, but I still have nice curves.

"It was so nice having you home for the weekend," my mother said over the phone. I promised I would call my parents as soon as I got home.

"Yes, it was a nice visit. I'm still upset Jonathan is taller than me."

"It was bound to happen, dear. He should end up at least six feet tall. He is in a real growth spurt right now."

"At least I still have an inch on Chelsea," I said.

"Maybe you can time your next visit for when she is home on break," my mother suggested.

"I'll be home for Thanksgiving."

"I'm going to hold you to that."

"Okay. I love you. Tell dad and Jonathan that I love them, too," I said.

"I will. We love you, too."

I hung up and thought about getting Kelly's old room rented. I had a great job in advertising at Jacobs & Sloane Advertising Agency, but there was no way I could swing the rent on my own. Not in Manhattan. I wondered if I could convince my best friend from work to move in with me.

Megan Barnes had become a great friend since we started working together at Jacobs & Sloane. We'd become like sisters over the past year and half. We even look very similar. Most people think we are sisters.

Megan was currently living with her boyfriend, but he was moving to London for a new job. He asked Megan to go with him but she hadn't given him an answer yet. She was torn, but I suspected she was leaning toward staying in New York. Her family was here and she loved her job at Jacobs & Sloane. She had a good relationship with Josh, but I didn't think it was at the point where she would move to another country for him.

I decided to give Megan a call.

"Hey Rache," Megan said when she answered her phone. Megan was the only person who called me Rache. I preferred Rachel, but gave up trying to correct Megan. It was a term of endearment and I was used to it from her.

"Hi, Megs," I replied. Her entire family and closest friends called her Megs.

"How was Boston?" she asked.

"Very nice. Kelly found a nice place. She can walk to her office."

"Sounds great. How is your family?"

"They are all doing great. Jonathan has shot up since I saw him last." I left out that he was now taller than me. I was still sore about that.

"Have you decided what to do about London?"

"I told Josh last night that I'm staying in New York," she said.

"How did he take it?"

"He was disappointed, but understood. I think we both knew that I'd decide to stay. He's a great guy, but it's not like we had reached a point in our relationship where either one of us moving for the other makes a whole lot of sense."

"Are you going to try the long distance relationship?"

"No. That's a bit sad, but I've realized the past few months that I don't see myself marrying him. A long distance relationship would be hard even under the best of circumstances. We've agreed to break up when he moves."

"I'm sorry, sweetie," I said.

"We're okay with it."

"Does this mean you will consider renting Kelly's old room?"

"I was hoping you would ask." I could feel Megan's smile through the phone.

"That is so awesome. It's going to be great having you live here."

"I know. I can't afford rent on my own and I like your place so much better than mine."

"Well, now you can start thinking of *my* place as *our* place," I said with a broad smile.

"Yippee! We can work out the details tomorrow."

"Okay. See you tomorrow, roomie."

"Later, roomie."

I was thrilled Megan would be moving in. It alleviated my concern about paying the rent and it would be so much fun sharing a place with her. No sooner had I tossed my iPhone onto the kitchen table then it started ringing. I checked the screen. Roger.

Roger was my boyfriend. At least I thought he was still my boyfriend. We had been dating about three months. Everything was going fine until he found out Kelly was moving out.

He immediately wanted to move in together. I told him I wasn't ready. We had a huge fight and hadn't spoken in two days.

I was surprised at our positions on the issue. I am all about commitment and a relationship. I eventually want the type of marriage my parents have. Roger was worth building a long-term relationship with, but I wasn't ready to commit to living together at this point in our relationship.

"Hi, Roger," I said as I answered the phone.

"Rachel, I'm sorry. I was wrong to get so upset about the whole not living together thing. You're right, we're not ready to take that step. I hope you still want to be with me."

"Yes. Apology accepted. And I'm sorry, too. I can definitely see how you could reasonably assume that living together would be something that I wanted. I am the queen of commitment and relationship."

"I thought asking you to move in together would prove I am committed to you and our relationship," Roger said.

"I realize that. As much as it is important to me, it's also important we don't rush into something we are not ready for."

"I get it. As long as we are good," said Roger.

"We're better than good," I replied.

CHAPTER 3

The Renauds had a great relationship with their bank. Within weeks the bank approved the financing needed. Andrew drew up all the legal paperwork and incorporated *Renaud's*. David called in a favor of an architect friend to assist in drawing up the designs according to Justin's vision. Matthew contacted the contractors he used at the hotel.

Justin had spoken to his mother and she was happy with her sons' decision. She knew how much Justin hated his job and dreamed of running a restaurant his way. It would also transform the old restaurant into something new. Wipe away the last reminder of her life with her ex-husband.

Justin was meeting with the architect to finalize the design of the restaurant. While the architect explained his ideas, he showed Justin how everything could be configured using the design software on his iPad.

"Perfect. Let's make it happen," replied Justin.

"Alright. I think I have everything I need. We'll finish these up and get them to the contractor," said the architect.

"Great."

Justin shook hands with the architect. He then surveyed the now empty space from the second floor balcony. The downstairs would have the main dining room and bar. The balcony was large enough for smaller tables which would offer a birds-eye view of the restaurant below.

Renaud's was now a legal entity and work was beginning. Soon it would be a new restaurant. Different from the one

Justin's father ran for so many years. Justin looked forward to starting a new chapter in his life.

CHAPTER 4

I sat in my office staring out the window at the building across the street. I was thinking about my situation with Roger. I didn't regret my decision about not moving in together. I was looking forward to Megan moving in with me, but my goal was to settle down and get married. *Could Roger be the one?*

"Knock, knock." I heard Charlie Jacobs voice behind me.

Charles, Charlie, Jacobs was the co-founder and president of Jacobs & Sloane. My boss. And a sweetheart of a man.

I spun around in my chair as Charlie stepped into my office. He plopped down in the chair in front of my desk. He had a broad smile across his face.

"I just wanted to stop by and tell you what an outstanding job you've been doing. Janice told me how invaluable you are to her team," he said.

"Thank you, Charlie," I said. Everybody called him Charlie. We were a small advertising agency. I decided on Jacobs & Sloane over the larger Manhattan ad agencies for that reason.

I saw more opportunity to contribute to campaigns and earn my own accounts sooner. I had also really hit it off with Charlie and the other staff when I interviewed with them. It was hard to believe that I had been at the company a year already.

"I wanted to let you know that we are promoting you to junior executive, effective immediately. You will take on increasingly larger roles on the accounts you work on. I suspect a year from now you will be heading your own accounts."

"Wow. I can't believe this. Thank you, Charlie. I won't disappoint you."

"I know you won't. Rachel, you deserve this promotion. You have worked hard and proven yourself immensely talented and more than capable to take on the greater responsibility. The promotion comes with a nice ten percent increase in your salary," Charlie said.

He could tell from the large smile on my face how happy I was with the news. I was anxious to contribute more of my ideas to shaping campaigns. Now I had my chance.

"Your first campaign as a junior executive will be Jacqueline magazine. Janice will fill you in on all the details, but it is one of our largest campaigns to date. Even though you are not heading the account, there is a lot of opportunity to leave your mark on the overall campaign. I think you will be perfect for it."

"I can't wait to get started on it," I said. I was still beaming. *Jacqueline* magazine was a leading fashion magazine and would be a real feather in my cap if I did a good job on the account.

"You'll do great. Congratulations, Rachel." Charlie then got up and headed out of my office.

"Thanks again!" I called to him as he exited.

He offered me another warm smile as he departed down the hall toward his office.

I walked down the hall to Megan's office. She had made junior executive last month. She felt a little bad telling me at the time as she thought I would be disappointed that we hadn't been promoted at the same time. But I was so happy for her when it happened. And I knew my promotion would come along eventually.

I nearly skipped down the hall as I couldn't wait to share the good news that I had been promoted. Megan was just hanging up the phone when I got to her office.

"It must be good news," she said as she looked up at me.

"I just made junior executive."

Megan jumped up and shrieked with joy. She threw her arms around me.

"That is great news! Congratulations, sweetie. You were overdue for that promotion," she said. "We have to celebrate tonight."

"Sounds like a plan," I said. "Dinner and drinks are on me. I want to spend a little of the raise."

"I know how you feel. The extra income is pretty sweet," replied Megan.

I knew that my raise was exactly the same as what she had received with her promotion. We had started at the same time and at the same salary. It was also no secret that the promotion to junior executive came with a ten percent raise.

"I'm going to call Roger and give him the good news," I said.

"Okay. Think about where we should go to celebrate."

"I will," I said. I headed back to my office and called Roger.

"That's great news, honey," he said when I told him about my promotion.

"Can you join Megan and me for a celebratory dinner?" I asked.

"Better than that," he said, "It will be my treat."

"See you tonight," I said.

"Later, beautiful."

CHAPTER 5

Megan, Roger, and I had a wonderful dinner. We ate at one of my favorite Italian restaurants. They have great food and I love their Chianti. I probably had a few too many glasses of Chianti as I had a slight buzz by the end of dinner. *But it's not everyday that you make junior executive*, I thought.

Roger and I dropped Megan off at her place. We still had a few months before Megan moved in with me. Josh was spending more time in London with his new job, but wouldn't move for two more months when their lease was up. I was a bit nervous about covering my rent on my own until then, but my raise would go a long way to help with that.

I tossed my keys and purse on the table by the door. Roger closed the door behind us as I clicked on a living room light. Roger reached over and pulled me toward him.

"Get over here, Ms. Junior Executive," he said as he wrapped his arms around my waist.

"Dinner was great. Thank you," I said as I gazed into his eyes.

Roger was five feet eleven inches with a slender but toned frame. He was a runner like me. We had met in a Central Park running club.

I was taken by his warm hazel eyes and kind smile. We met over the summer and his blond hair was very light from the sun. It was a darker blond now that we were into the fall. He had soft, supple lips and was an amazing kisser.

"You are very welcome. The least I could do to celebrate your promotion."

I tilted my head upward and kissed him. Our lips were sweet from the Chianti.

"This has been a great three months," commented Roger.

That was true. But there was something about his tone that troubled me.

"Why did you say it like that? Is there a 'but' coming that I am not going to like?" I asked with concern.

CHAPTER 6

"I guess that depends," Roger finally said.

"On what?"

"On how you feel about a new opportunity."

"Roger, don't beat around the bush. Tell me exactly what is going on."

"I just found out today that my company is transferring me to Dallas."

"Dallas? Why? Do you have a say in this?"

"It would be a promotion. They want me to serve as the lead data analyst for the entire southwest region."

Roger was a data scientist. I didn't fully understand his job, but he had degrees in statistics and computer programming. He was one of those guys looking at "Big Data" and helped his company understand customer behavior.

I didn't know what to say. It was obviously a step up for Roger in his career. How could I be against his advancement after we just celebrated my promotion? But Dallas was a pretty long way from New York City. If I really meant that much to him, wouldn't he put the company off for a little while longer? Had my not moving in with him nudged him in this direction?

"Roger, that's great. For your career, I mean. And you deserve it. I'm happy about that. But what does that mean for us?"

"I guess we need to figure it out," he said. "I can't pass up this opportunity. At my company, you either move up or die on the vine where you are. Plus, I'd be making more money and the cost of living is a lot less in Dallas compared to Manhattan."

"You've already decided to go, haven't you?"

I already knew the answer to my question. If Roger wasn't taking the job, we wouldn't even be having the conversation.

"I know the timing stinks, but this could be a good thing for us," Roger said earnestly. "I know you don't want to live together, but Dallas is insanely cheap compared to Manhattan. Heck, I could afford a place for each of us while you try to get another position. With your experience . . ."

I cut him off. "Wait a minute, why should I be the one to give up my job? Especially after I just got promoted?"

Roger's face hardened a bit. "But you don't have a problem with me giving up my promotion so that I can stay here? When you are not sure if you want to be committed to me enough to live together?"

"Roger, you know my decision to not live with you now has absolutely nothing to do with my commitment to you. Don't even go there!" I said angrily.

"Okay, okay!" Roger muttered, relenting. "Look, I don't want to fight with you over this. I know it seems like a sudden thing, but think about how great it could be. You could have an amazing apartment nicer than anything here in Manhattan. I've spent days researching the housing market and I could even buy a house right off the bat with the raise the company is giving me. Because I'm moving into management I'm getting a twenty percent increase in salary."

I stared at Roger, watching what could have been a great relationship dissolving quickly in front of me. Did he seriously think I was going to give up my career to move across the country? If he really wanted things to work, couldn't he compromise with the company?

"But that just proves my point," I said carefully. "If they like you so much, then surely they'll agree to let you wait a bit. Why not go back and say you'd like to wait six months? That gives us time to figure out where things are between us. And you are so talented they'll probably offer you something better in Manhattan."

I smiled, feeling clever at my plan. But Roger apparently didn't agree because he looked angry.

"You're not really listening to me," Roger said. "My career would take a nosedive if I turned down this position. Not to mention I would be an idiot to turn down a twenty percent increase in pay. I'll finally be able to pay off my student loans. And not have to live in a tiny apartment."

I fought back tears. "So what you're saying is the money outweighs a chance at a relationship with us?" I asked.

I knew I was being unreasonable, but I was upset.

"What about you?" Roger asked. "Why don't you ask your employer for a six-month leave and move with me to Dallas? I can afford to pay all your expenses even if you don't work at all."

I gaped at him. "And lose all my client contacts? Do you really think they would allow me to do that? My boss is finally giving me more responsibility. Do you know how hard it can be for a woman to advance?"

Roger suddenly dropped his head. "Look at us. We're already tearing each other apart."

I began to cry. Roger was a great guy. I really could see a future with him. But he was asking me to give up a career and move across the country where I would have no friends, no family, and no job. We just weren't far enough into our relationship for me to make such a drastic change in my life.

Roger drew me close and hugged me. My tears streamed down my face and onto his chest. I wondered how many more times he would be able to hold me. How many more times would we be together like that. But to be honest, I was still reeling. Part of me just couldn't comprehend why he wouldn't try a bit harder to stay here in Manhattan.

I understood he had a great opportunity. But he was in a high demand field. Several companies in New York had competed to hire him for this current position. I just didn't believe he was worried about job prospects if he refused the move. And I still suspected my not moving in with him was impacting his decision.

"I'm sorry, Rachel. I didn't go looking for the job. You know how much I want to be with you."

I pulled my head back and wiped the tears from my eyes. Now doubt had entered my mind and I wasn't sure how much Roger wanted to be with me.

"When will you move?"

"Four weeks. The company is going to take care of the remainder of my lease here until we can get my apartment rented. They're putting me up in a corporate apartment in Dallas until I find a place to live there."

"So this move is pretty permanent?"

"Looks that way. The Dallas office is really growing so I'll have more opportunity for further advancement."

Obviously, Roger had already settled this move in his mind. This talk was simply a way to inform me of what he had already planned out in great detail. I suddenly wondered why I was only hearing of this promotion now. Hadn't Roger said he had researched the housing markets already? Surely he wouldn't have had time to do that today? The other stuff regarding his lease sounded complicated as well.

Had the company really had time to offer the position, wait for his decision, and then make all these very detailed arrangements? Was it really coincidence he got a promotion the exact same day as me?

"I guess the only question left is what we're going to do about us?" Roger said.

"I don't see how we could make a long distance relationship work," I said, my voice dull.

"I figured as much. What do you want to do? We still have a few weeks. Or is it easier to say goodbye now?"

Even with my current anger, I didn't want to say goodbye so suddenly. But I wondered if it would be harder if we waited. Maybe I needed to handle this like removing a bandage. A quick clean break hurt more right away, but then you could move on from it sooner.

"I don't know. Just hold me for now," I said as I leaned into him. Roger wrapped his arms around me. I rested against his chest and listened to his heart beat. I wanted to stay like that forever, but knew it would end. I could feel the tears welling up in my eyes again.

CHAPTER 7

14 Months Later

It had been more than a year since Roger moved to Dallas. We decided we couldn't stand the thought of ending our relationship abruptly. We saw each other a few more times to say our goodbyes.

He and I kept in touch for a few months after he moved. Roger eventually met someone else. I've dated, but nothing serious.

On the plus side, Megan and I had been sharing the apartment for a year. It had been a great year from that perspective. I loved having Megan as my roommate.

I had also grown into my role as a junior executive at Jacobs and Sloane. The Jacqueline magazine account had consumed about ninety percent of my time at work over the past year. Even though I wasn't heading the account, I had a lot of creative input.

Ashley Sullivan, the Director of Social Media at Davenport Media, which owned the magazine, was fantastic to work with. She understood social media and the fashion industry like no one else I had ever met. Ashley was a young executive, like myself, and soon discovered we had much in common. She even invited me for cocktails with Brandon Mitchell, the CEO of Davenport Media, and Jacqueline Davenport, the owner and President of Davenport Media and the magazine's namesake.

I was in awe of Jacqueline Davenport who was smart and sophisticated. Brandon Mitchell had to be one of the most handsome men on the planet. He and Ashley were clearly an item and they looked great together. I was having a wonderful time with the ad campaign and it was going very well.

Megan had received her first lead account last month and was busy guiding the work of that campaign. I was told I would be getting my own account soon. Charlie was looking for just the perfect campaign for me to take the lead on. Business was good, so I knew it was a matter of time before the "perfect" account walked through the doors of Jacobs & Sloane.

I was taking a mental break from my work and checking Facebook. Roger had posted a picture of him with his new girlfriend at a Dallas Cowboys game. She was pretty and they looked happy. It still hurt a little. I was happy for Roger but I wanted what he had.

Had Roger been the only man in Manhattan that I could have a relationship with? I knew that wasn't true. Although with each passing month I did ask myself the question more and more.

Megan walked into my office and slid into the chair across from my desk.

"I know the look," she said.

"What look," I said trying to deny I had a look.

"The look that says you are lonely for a man in your life."

"*Lonely* may be too strong."

Megan tilted her had and gave me a *who are you trying to fool?* look.

"Okay. Maybe I'm approaching *lonely*."

"Rache, there is a simple cure for what you have," said Megan.

"I'm well aware of that. But if it were simple for me, I wouldn't be in the situation I find myself in."

"I can't help you if you won't first help yourself," said Megan as if she were my therapist.

I rolled my eyes and glanced back at my computer screen. Roger and his lovely girlfriend were staring back at me from my Facebook news feed.

"Is it too much to ask that I find one decent guy who at least has relationship potential?"

"Maybe you are too picky. Maybe you need to be willing to take a little more of a chance in the beginning."

"What, like throwing caution to the wind?"

"Something like that. Well, I gotta run to a meeting. Will you be ready at six to head home?"

"Yeah. Six is fine," I said.

"Think about what I said," Megan said as she exited my office.

I had no idea what the outcome would be, but I was beginning to think something had to give. I had wanted a man just like Roger. I was starting to rethink how much like Roger he needed to be. Maybe I needed to be more open about the next guy. I wanted to find "Mr. Right," but maybe "Mr. Close Enough" would suffice. Maybe he would even turn out to be "Mr. Right" in the end.

CHAPTER 8

"Well, little bro, we're getting close," said Andrew as he clapped Justin on the shoulders.

"Finally. It has taken much too long," replied Justin.

The process of opening *Renaud's* took several months longer than Justin had anticipated. Between building permits, construction issues during remolding, obtaining liquor licenses, hiring staff, and a million other little things Justin couldn't even recall, it had been a long year. Now *Renaud's* was just a day away from the grand opening.

All the frustrations and hard work were worth it. Justin looked out over the restaurant from the second floor balcony. He was very happy with what he saw. It matched his vision perfectly. The space looked nothing like the old family restaurant.

The only remaining issue was the advertising campaign. Justin felt it lacked the punch it needed.

They had been using the same firm Matthew's hotel used. It was one of the large Madison Avenue advertising agencies. They were excellent. But corporate. Justin wanted to go a different route.

He wanted his restaurant to be sophisticated. He didn't feel Matthew's advertising agency understood his vision very well. He had recently seen an ad for *Jacqueline* magazine that was sophisticated in just the way he wanted to advertise the restaurant.

He learned Jacobs & Sloane Advertising Agency developed the campaign. That was who he wanted to handle the restaurant's campaign. He looked them up online and called to set up a meeting.

"I know we are stuck with the ads we have for the grand opening, but I want a different campaign going forward," Justin told Andrew.

"Well, we all decided you managing the restaurant day-to-day meant you have responsibility for those type of decisions. What are you thinking?"

"Have you seen the Jacqueline magazine ads?" Justin asked.

"Yeah. Who hasn't? They've blitzed the Manhattan market the past several months."

"Exactly. And the sophistication they convey is exactly what I want."

"It's a good campaign. Do you know who put it together?"

"A small firm. Jacobs & Sloane. I have a meeting with Charles Jacobs this afternoon."

"Let me know how it goes," said Andrew. "I have some papers to file with the court for one of my clients. I'll talk to you later."

"See ya," said Justin. He watched Andrew wind down the circular staircase and cross the first floor of the restaurant.

"Hey, Drew!" Justin called out to his brother.

Andrew stopped and turned around. He looked up at Justin.

"Tomorrow night, this place will be jammed! It's going to be awesome! Just wait and see!"

Andrew smiled and waved at Justin. "I know! We've got you running the place!" he yelled back.

Justin smiled. He was going to put *Renaud's* on the map. He checked his watch and saw it was time to leave for his meeting with Charles Jacobs at Jacobs & Sloane.

CHAPTER 9

"Mr. Renaud, please come in," said Charlie Jacobs as he greeted Justin in the reception area of Jacobs & Sloane Advertising Agency.

"Please, call me Justin."

"Very well. Everyone calls me Charlie. Right this way."

Charlie walked Justin back to his office. They sat at a small conference table.

"Can we get you anything to drink?" asked Charlie.

"No, thank you."

"I understand you are about to have the grand opening for your new restaurant. Congratulations."

"Yes. Tomorrow night. Thank you. My brothers and I are excited."

"I've seen the ads for your opening. They are quite good. I know the folks at your current agency. They do good work."

"Yes. The issue is not with the quality of the work nor with the agency itself. The hotel one of my brothers manages uses them and they are very effective for them. But the hotel caters to the corporate crowd. Renaud's is a completely different animal. I just don't feel they are capturing the essence of my restaurant."

"If you don't mind, can you say a little bit more about that?"

"Well, *Renaud's* offers a sophisticated dining experience for young professionals living in Manhattan."

"We have a few campaigns expressing something similar. One, in particular, wanted us to capture the essence of *sophistication*. Not unlike what you are looking for."

"Exactly. I assume you are referring to the Jacqueline magazine ads," said Justin.

"Yes. It has been a great campaign for us," answered Charlie.

"Indeed. That campaign is why I am here speaking with you. That is the type of campaign I want for Renaud's. I believe whoever worked on that campaign can effectively create a campaign for me."

"We have an excellent team working on that campaign. It is headed by Janice Reynolds, but much of the creative force behind the ads is Rachel Cooper. She is one of our most promising junior executives. I think she would be excellent to head your account. Assuming, of course, you decide to hire us for the campaign."

"I'd like to hear some of Ms. Cooper's ideas, but if they are anything like the Jacqueline magazine campaign then I see no reason why Jacobs & Sloane will not be my new advertising agency."

"Rachel is at a meeting out of the office, but I will have her contact you as soon as she gets back to set up an appointment with you."

"I look forward to meeting her."

"Excellent. Why don't we go over how we establish accounts here at Jacobs & Sloane."

Charlie and Justin discussed the details of establishing an account at the agency and their fees. Charlie also got a better idea of the types of creatives Justin was looking for in his campaign. At the end of the meeting, Justin noticed they passed by Rachel Cooper's office.

The door to her office was closed and the lights were off. He couldn't tell much from a closed office, but he wondered about Rachel Cooper. She was a junior executive so he figured she was young. Around his age, he figured.

Justin was looking forward to meeting the creative force behind the Jacqueline magazine campaign. He wanted to know if she was as sophisticated as the ads she designed. He imagined she must be. Justin was very much looking forward to meeting Rachel Cooper.

CHAPTER 10

Justin Renaud

I stood up from the table after finishing my dessert.

"Where are you going?" asked Sarah. Or was it Susan?

"I have an afternoon meeting to discuss the advertising campaign for my restaurant."

"Just a little while longer?" she whined as she finished her slice of cheesecake. I hate whining. I also hate when a woman acts desperate.

"Maybe next week," I said.

"Okay. You'll call me?"

"If I have time next week."

"Didn't you have a nice time?"

Oh jeez. Did she really need my validation? Every once in a while I got a self-doubter like Sarah, or whatever her name is.

"I gotta run. The bill is paid, including the tip. But stay as long as you like."

I exited the cafe and closed the door behind me. I felt a little bad for her. But I'm always up front with a woman before I go on a date. I was honest with her . . . yes, Sarah is her name – Like the Hall & Oates song.

Some people would say I'm a jerk when it comes to women. An arrogant jerk. Maybe I am. But the women I date never complain. They always want to see me again. Sounds bad, I know.

Nonetheless, despite being indifferent as to who I am with on a date – and being dead set against committing to any woman, I am a gentleman. I treat my dates with respect, I take them to the finest restaurants, and offer interesting conversation. I also let them know I'm happy to take them out, but I'm not looking to settle down. Some women are okay with this – or think they will change me and I will fall head over heels in love with them.

Others turn heel and walk away as fast as possible – not wanting to waste their time on a guy who won't even entertain committing to a relationship. I get it. I'm just not the kind of guy to want a relationship. And for good reason. My parents had a terrible marriage and a nasty divorce. A lot of my friends have parents who are also divorced. I don't need that. My way is easier – uncomplicated.

I want to focus on my new restaurant. Running a business is tough enough. I don't need a relationship to complicate my life. I certainly don't need the type of relationship my parents had.

I hailed a cab. I only had a half hour before my meeting. Rachel Cooper from Jacobs & Sloane advertising agency was coming by the restaurant to go over the new ad campaign. We spoke on the phone and she had a great voice. I looked up her profile on the Jacobs and Sloane website and she looked cute in her picture.

The prospect of dating a business associate probably wasn't advisable. But I always found a way to get what I wanted. I decided to keep my options open.

CHAPTER 11

"Rachel Cooper, you rock! I just heard you are heading the Renaud's restaurant account," said my best friend Megan as she walked into my office. Megan and I are advertising representatives at Jacob and Sloane Advertising agency.

"Wow. Word travels fast."

"It is a big deal. Your first lead account," said Megan as she plopped down in the chair next to my desk. "Is that what you are going to wear to your meeting at the restaurant?" Megan asked as she looked over my outfit.

"Yes. Why? What's wrong with it?"

"Nothing. If you were trying out for a role in sisters of the traveling pantsuits."

Megan and I started at Jacobs & Sloane the same week. We served on our very first account together and became fast friends. She is pretty, smart, and can be wickedly funny.

"Megs, there is nothing wrong with a pantsuit for business."

"I didn't say there was. I'm just saying you need to dress for the client. Your client is Justin Renaud of *Renaud's*, not the Secretary of State."

Megan had a point. Justin Renaud was very handsome and looked like he belonged on the cover of GQ.

"Okay. Any suggestions?" I said.

"You have great legs and a cute butt. You definitely need to wear a skirt that shows them off. I think I know which of your outfits would be perfect."

Megan was more of a fashionista than I am. She's been a great help in picking out just the right outfit to match the occasion.

I don't eat as healthily as I would like. That is a hazard of my profession given the long hours and often being on the run to meetings with clients. All-in-all though, I strike a quite good pose. And, I have Megan. She always finds a way to boost my appeal for dates.

"I knew you would," I said with a smile. "How about we grab lunch and swing by the apartment so I can change before the meeting? It's on the way to the restaurant."

"Sounds like a plan," said Megan as she hopped out of her chair.

Once we were settled in a cab, Megan whipped out her iPad.

"Have you seen the latest article on Justin Renaud?" asked Megan as she pulled up *The New York Times* web page.

"No. What does it say?"

"It's a society piece. Talks about his background and the opening of the restaurant." She handed me her iPad when she located the article.

"Nice picture of him," I commented as she handed me her iPad.

"I don't think he takes a bad picture," she replied. "The article says he is a confirmed bachelor and does not have a steady girlfriend."

"I don't see how that is relevant," I said rather dismissively.

"Really? You don't?"

"No. I don't"

"Rache, he's so cute. How can you not be thinking about that when you are less than three hours from meeting with him?"

A few things about Megan. First, she is the only person who calls me *Rache* and gets away with it. I prefer Rachel, but I gave up correcting Megan. It is a term of endearment from her and I have learned to be okay with it. Second, Megan is always on the prowl for a good-looking guy. And she thinks I should be as well.

"Yes, Justin Renaud is handsome. But this is a business meeting. He is a client. It would be unprofessional to flirt with him."

"Ugh. You and your business ethics."

"Megs, you know I'm right."

"I suppose. But you should feel out the situation. Who knows, he may invite something more than just business."

I emailed the article link to myself. I knew Megan wasn't going to give me the opportunity to actually read the article in the cab. I handed her iPad back to her.

"I'll take it under advisement," I said.

"See that you do," she said.

We pulled up in front of our apartment building. I was glad to pay the driver and get out of the cab before Megan said anything else. We went upstairs and Megan headed straight to her bedroom.

"Let me show you the outfit I have in mind. It will be perfect."

Megan and I were almost the exact same size, so we often shared outfits. We actually looked a lot alike. She had lighter brown hair than me and blue eyes. Other than that, we could easily be confused for one another. Most people thought we were sisters.

"Okay. Just remember to keep it appropriate for a business meeting," I reminded Megan.

There was part of me looking forward to appearing more fetching than usual for a business meeting. At the same time I didn't want to be unprofessional. I certainly did not want to send the wrong message to Justin Renaud. Even if he was extremely handsome.

CHAPTER 12

Megan selected a black Sakkas Knee Length Tiered Sleek Stretch Skirt. It flattered my figure in showing my curves and legs. I picked a white blouse that did not reveal cleavage, but formed nicely to my torso. Megan approved and I had my fetching and professional outfit.

I gave a final review of my *Renaud's* file on the cab ride over to the restaurant. When we pulled up, I was impressed with the entrance. It was modern and understated. The sign above the doors was in a simple, bold script. Everything about the entrance stated that this was a modern, sophisticated, and upscale restaurant. From a marketing perspective, I'd give the first impression as an A+.

I opened the front door and entered the restaurant. It was empty except for a bartender and a few of the wait staff setting up for the evening.

The restaurant, like the front entrance, was modern and sleek. There was a long bar at the end that was black with a glass top. There was a large, fully stocked, wine rack behind the bar.

I walked over to the bar and introduced myself. "Hello. I'm Rachel Cooper, with Jacobs & Sloane. I have an appointment with Mr. Renaud."

"Hi, I'm Nick," replied the bartender. "Justin is in his office. I'll let him know you are here."

Nick picked up the phone and punched in an extension. "Justin, a Ms. Rachel Cooper from Jacob & Sloane is here." He paused for a moment and then said, "Okay," before he hung up. He turned back toward me.

"Justin will be down in just a minute," Nick said. "Can I get you anything? It's on the house."

"Sparkling water would be great."

"Coming right up." Nick went to the back of the bar and returned with a bottle of sparkling water and a glass. He poured the water and slid the glass in front of me.

"Thank you," I said.

Justin Renaud appeared from the back of the balcony and made his way down the spiral staircase. He moved with a swagger which told you he was confident and in control. I couldn't quite decide if it also bordered on arrogant. As he approached I could see how good looking he really was.

Justin Renaud stood slightly more than six feet tall with an athletic build. He had short brown hair. He had the brooding good looks of a handsome face with luscious lips. His light brown eyes drew me into his stare.

"Ms. Cooper, Justin Renaud. It is a pleasure to meet you," he said as he extended his hand.

"It is nice to meet you, Mr. Renaud," I replied as I shook his hand.

"Justin, please."

"Rachel."

"Why don't we have a seat upstairs? It offers the best view of the restaurant," he said as he helped me down from the stool.

He looked me over as I hopped down. He wasn't ogling me in a creepy way, but he wasn't discrete either. I got the distinct impression he had perfected sizing a woman up within a few seconds. *What does he think?* I thought to myself.

Justin gave no signal one way or the other. Whatever he thought, he wasn't showing it. He let go of my hand as soon as I was standing.

"Right this way, Rachel," he said as he directed me toward the staircase.

The stairs were wide, but I was glad I wore flats. I hated climbing stairs in heels. As we climbed the stairs, my woman's intuition told me Justin was checking me out from behind. To be honest, I would have checked out his backside if I were given the opportunity.

"How about here?" Justin asked as we reached the top of the stairs. We sat at one of the tables which offered a sweeping view of the restaurant below.

Justin unbuttoned his suit jacket and sat down across from me. He was impeccably dressed in a designer suit and crisp shirt, opened at the collar. He tugged on one of his French cuffs as stretched his arms out and placed them on the table.

I reminded myself this was a business meeting, but Justin Renaud looked so attractive. I gained my composure and looked him in the eyes. Those dreamy brown eyes were breathtaking.

I excused myself to go to the ladies room. I splashed cold water on my face and took a few deep breaths. "What the . . ." I said to myself in the mirror. "Come on Rachel. Get a grip. You have work to do." My reflection didn't have any more words of wisdom.

I dried my face and touched up my makeup. I took another deep breath and exhaled. This was my first lead account. I needed to do a good job. *Focus!* I returned to the table.

"I'd love to learn more about the restaurant and show you what I have worked up so far," I said as I sat back down.

"Excellent," replied Justin as he leaned forward for a better look at my iPad. He smelled as delicious as he looked. This was going to be harder than I thought.

CHAPTER 13

I cleared my throat. I confirmed the details Justin had discussed with Charlie Jacobs. I then showed him the draft concept for the ad campaign.

"I love what you have already," Justin said. "I obviously made the correct choice in hiring Jacobs & Sloane. And I am certainly glad you are handling the account."

He flashed a smile that made me melt inside.

"Thank you. Of course I will need more details so I can flesh out the basic concept."

"Sounds like we may need to spend some considerable time together."

Justin flashed me another smile. He had a great smile. It was hypnotic and he used it effectively.

I might have blushed. I felt flushed. *Is he hitting on you?* I thought.

"I'm sure we can come up with the creatives without taking too much of your time."

"I wouldn't mind if you did take up a lot of my time. Provided it is you I will be meeting with."

Okay. That's a bit more direct.

"Well, I am heading this account. So, yes, I would be your point of contact. And, naturally, we will spend whatever time you feel is necessary to nail the concept."

Justin pursed his lips. *Oh my gosh.* What incredible pink lips he had. So full and moist. I could almost sense his lips on mine. *Get it together, Rachel! How can you be thinking about kissing a client?*

My throat felt dry. I took a drink of sparkling water. It gave me a moment to think of what to say next.

"Renaud is French? Is that how you came up with *Renaud's* for the restaurant's name?" I finally asked.

"Yes. My grandparents, on my father's side, came to America from Quebec, Canada. Perhaps a bit cliché, but my grandfather was a pastry chef. He worked in some of the finest restaurants and hotels in New York City."

"Do you mind if I take some notes? You never know when a piece of the history will spark an idea for the campaign."

"No. I don't mind at all."

"Please, continue."

Justin sat back in his chair. He had a confident air about him. Yes, his swagger from earlier was one of confidence.

"The Renaud surname is one of rich and dynamic history," Justin continued. "It is of Germanic origin from when the Visigoths controlled France from the mid-fifth to early eighth centuries and comes from a personal name meaning 'counsel' and 'rule'. My ancestors settled in Quebec around the mid-seventeenth century until my grandfather came to New York in the twentieth century."

"Very interesting," I commented with a warm a smile.

"The rest of my family's genealogy in America is rather unremarkable. What may be of interest is I have three brothers. We are all two years apart. I'm the youngest. We are partners in the restaurant, along with a few investors."

"So, *Renaud's* is a bit of a family business?"

"Yes and no. My brothers are more silent partners."

"Is the style of the restaurant your vision?" I asked.

"Yes. I want *Renaud's* to be a place where young professionals can come to let loose from the workday. A restaurant where they can have a few superb drinks, mingle with a sophisticated clientele, and enjoy a great meal with friends."

Justin paused a moment and leaned forward. He placed his arms on the table. He looked directly at me. Again with those dreamy brown eyes.

"Have you ever felt a sense of overpowering emotion? A sudden, intense feeling where you are surrounding by elegance?"

"I, um . . ." I stammered.

I gave up trying to form words. I simply smiled and glanced down at my iPad. I needed to end the meeting and get out before something happened I would regret. Maybe I wouldn't regret it, but I knew it wouldn't be professional.

"I think I have some good information," I finally stated. "I will get to work on a more complete ad campaign workup to show you." I closed my iPad case, gathered my file and purse, and stood up.

"Thank you for your time, Justin."

"No. Thank you. I appreciate you coming by the restaurant to meet. I will show you out."

He placed his hand gently on the small of my back as we turned toward the stairs. A jolt of electricity shot through my entire body. My legs felt like rubber bands. I steeled myself to keep upright.

When we reached the front door, Justin shook my hand. "Thank you again. I look forward to seeing the full campaign," he said as he opened the door for me.

"I will be in touch soon."

"Excellent," he replied as I stepped through the open door.

"You know," he said before I reached the sidewalk. "You should really come by the restaurant one evening. Take in the full experience."

"That sounds like a good idea. It might help with my creativity for the campaign."

"You have an open invitation as my guest. Your name will be on my personal VIP list."

"Thank you."

"And a plus one as well," he said. "I can't imagine there isn't someone in your life."

I giggled out of nervousness. "If you mean a boyfriend. No, not at present. But my best friend would love to tag along."

"Great."

I got the sense he was more responding to my not having a boyfriend than he was to Megan tagging along. But I tried not to dwell on it. We said goodbye and I hailed a taxi for a ride back to the office.

What was I getting myself into?

CHAPTER 14

Megan followed me into my office. "How did it go?" she asked excitedly. I swear Megan was part blood hound. At least when it came to sniffing out romantic tension.

"Interesting."

"How so?"

I shut my office door.

"I think Justin Renaud was flirting with me."

"Really? Do tell."

I told Megan about my meeting. What was said. How it was said. The vibe I was getting during our interaction.

"Yep. He was definitely flirting with you." Megan confirmed when I finished talking.

Not that I needed much confirmation. I may have been in a dry spell, a long dry spell, but I could still recognize being hit on.

"So, what are you going to do?" she asked.

"I don't know. I mean, I can't risk the account. I've never gotten involved with a client before. I'm not sure it's right."

Megan rolled her eyes. She had much lower standards when it came to client relations. Not that she had ever dated a client. Then again, she never had a client like Justin Renaud. Had it been Megan at today's meeting, she'd already have a date on her calendar.

"We need to at least check out the restaurant. See what happens. I've been wanting to go anyway," said Megan.

"I'll think about it."

"Rache, if you don't go he will be offended. You need to at least think about not offending your client."

"I don't think he would drop the agency if I failed to show up at *Renaud's* for dinner."

"Do you want to even take a chance?"

Megan had ulterior motives, but she made a valid point. Could I just ignore Justin's invitation? Would I do that to any other client? No. I wouldn't.

"Fine. We'll go Friday night," I relented.

"That's my girl," said Megan with a broad smile.

"Now get out. I have work to do," I said, waving Megan toward the door.

"Okay, I'm going. Swing by my office when you are ready to go home."

She exited my office and I tilted back in my chair.

"Knock, knock," said Charlie Jacobs.

"Hi, Mr. Jacobs," I said as he entered my office.

"How did your meeting go with Justin Renaud?"

"Just fine. We got along well and he provided some useful background I can use to round out the campaign."

"Excellent. I knew you would be perfect this campaign. Let me know when you have everything ready. I'd like to take a look before it is presented to Mr. Renaud."

"Yes, sir. I should have something by the end of next week."

"Good. Rachel, if all goes well with this account, the sky is the limit for you. There are a number of exciting accounts we are working on landing. I can definitely see you taking on a few of them."

"Thank you, Mr. Jacobs. I appreciate your confidence in me."

"Well, you've earned it. Just focus on the *Renaud's* account and then we'll talk."

Mr. Jacobs offered a warm smile and then left my office. I was jumping for joy inside. I had worked my ass off the past two years and it was paying off, big time. I spun around in my chair. I was determined this campaign would be a home run. Despite my better judgment, maybe in more ways than one.

CHAPTER 15

As Friday night arrived I was questioning if going to *Renaud's* was a good idea after all. I had gotten so hot and bothered around Justin during our meeting. I wasn't at all sure that I would be able to control myself around him in a more social atmosphere.

Megan, as usual, was able to talk me down from my near hysteria. In the end, we were dressed for a night on the town. And we looked great.

I was wearing a dress by Opening Ceremony. It was a white stretch knit dress with cap sleeves and a sweetheart neckline. It boasted a pencil skirt in mid-length.

"That is an awesome outfit," exclaimed Megan. "Really shows your figure."

"Thanks. I think I'll pair it with these earrings and purse," I said as I showed her my designer earrings and Whiting & Davis clutch.

"Perfect," she said.

"You are looking really amazing yourself," I said to Megan. She was wearing a black Elizabeth and James dress. The fabric was stretch crepe with sheer short sleeves with solid black cuffs. The dress emphasized a crew neckline and the fitted skirt showed off her great legs. She looked fetching in the dress.

We finished our makeup and headed out to *Renaud's*. As we pulled up front there was already a line around the corner.

"If this is the crowd now, imagine what it will be after your ad campaign," said Megan as we exited the taxi.

We approached a man at the front of the line who was the size of the Empire State Building. I gave him my name. He checked his tablet and waived Megan and me through.

"Did you notice all the looks we got?" asked Megan.

"They were probably just jealous that we were on the VIP list and got to go right in."

"Some of them, maybe. But most of the guys were checking us out. Face it Rache, we are two attractive girls at the most sophisticated new restaurant in Manhattan."

Renaud's was packed with many young, good-looking professionals. I noticed Nick and the other bartenders working feverishly to keep up with drink orders at the bar.

"Come on, let's get a cocktail," said Megan as she took me by the arm and pulled me toward the bar.

"Hi, Ms. Cooper," said Nick as he recognized me. "What can I get for you?"

"Hi, Nick. We'll have two appletinis," I replied.

Nick mixed us two drinks and placed them on the bar in front of me. They were colorful and looked great. I handed Nick some cash and he waved it away.

"You're Justin's guest. Everything's on the house."

Even so, I left Nick a tip.

"Thanks," he said. "I appreciate it."

It was nice of Justin to provide drinks on the house, but I didn't want to pick Nick's pocket as a result.

I took a sip of my appletini. It tasted as good as it looked.

"That is our top seller," I heard Justin's voice next to me.

"Justin. Hello. I can taste why. It's delicious." I turned toward him.

"I'm glad that you came. You look incredible," he said as he kissed my hand.

"Thank you. And thank you for having us as your guests. Justin, this is my friend Megan Barnes. Megan, this is Justin Renaud."

"Very nice to meet you, Megan."

"The pleasure is all mine," said Megan.

"So, what do you think?" asked Justin.

"I think you are doing an incredible job. To be honest, I'm not really sure why you need Jacobs & Sloane to run an advertising campaign for you. It looks like you're doing just fine already."

"We are off to a good start. But the initial hype will cool soon enough. I need you to keep us top of mind as the hottest restaurant."

Megan was already flirting with one of the cute guys next to us at the bar.

"It looks like *Renaud's* suits your friend," said Justin as he nodded toward Megan and her new friend.

"No offense, but any restaurant with cute guys suits Megan. But the cute guys here are probably more educated and higher on the pay scale than her typical pickup."

"So, a step up for her." He flashed me his winning smile.

"Why don't we have a seat at my private booth?"

"That sounds nice."

"Nick, please send a scotch and another appletini over to over to my table."

"You got it, boss," replied Nick.

Justin led me to a booth in the corner of the restaurant. It had beautiful leather seats and the same stylish glass top as the bar. We sat and a waitress brought over our drinks.

"Thank you, Wendy," said Justin as she placed the drinks on the table.

I took a sip from my new glass. I had to admit that I loved the drink. I needed to be careful, though. A few more of these and I'd be passed out on the table.

"To be honest, I wasn't sure I would ever see you at the restaurant socially," said Justin.

"Why do you say that?"

"Well, you were a little flustered the other day. Not professionally. You have the ad campaign well under control."

"That only leaves personally," I replied.

"It does," said Justin as he eased back in his seat.

"So you're saying I appeared flustered with you on a personal basis?"

"Not appeared. You were flustered. But it was very endearing."

Okay, now I was reconsidering the whole swagger thing. Maybe it was more arrogant than confident.

"Excuse me?" I realized that my tone was a bit indignant. But what was up with this guy all of a sudden?

"I didn't mean to upset you, Rachel. I'm just making conversation."

Justin was as casual and relaxed as could be. He almost seemed to relish I was working myself up.

"Pointing out a woman got all flustered around you is not 'just making conversation'," I said.

"Would it have helped if I had prefaced it by saying that I found it cute? That I find you extremely attractive?"

"No. It wouldn't. Do you really think this conversation is appropriate?"

"That depends."

"On what?"

"If your being flustered the other day is because you are attracted to me."

What?! I couldn't believe he just went there. It didn't matter there was some truth to it. His comment was way out of line.

"Mr. Renaud, I think we need to change the topic of this conversation."

"We are back to being formal?"

"I think it is best if we keep our interactions strictly professional. I appreciate you inviting me as your guest, but I think that is where we need to leave it."

Justin was extremely handsome. Truths be told, from a purely physical point of view, I was crazy not to express interest in his advances. But he was coming off as an arrogant jerk.

I grabbed my purse and slid toward the end of the booth to get up. Justin reached out and placed his hand on my forearm.

"Rachel, please don't go. You and I will both regret it if you do." He then removed his hand from my arm.

"Is that a threat to fire me from the account? Or fire Jacobs & Sloane?" I asked.

"No. That's business. This is personal."

"And exactly why would we regret my leaving?"

"Because we might miss out on something special."

"You really think it is that easy? I'd say you are supremely confident, but another word comes to mind."

Justin smiled at me.

"I think it is best if I leave," I said as I spun around and started to walk away.

"Rachel!" he called out to me. "You will change your mind."

I stopped in mid step and whirled back around. My nostrils flared with anger.

"You are so great you can predict the future?"

Justin shook his head and chuckled. He was smug. A smug, arrogant, jerk.

"In a way, yes. Rachel, past behavior can be an excellent predictor of future behavior."

"You and I have no past behavior," I protested.

"You and I don't. But I've been in this situation before."

I probably should have just kept walking. But I had this thing where I had to have the last word. I had to prove my point.

"Do you think bragging about women falling all over you makes me want to be with you more? Or you can assume I am anything like those other women?"

"Rachel, you are not like those other women. But things are still very much in my favor."

"Dream on!" I turned and moved quickly out of ear shot of Justin's voice.

If he said anything else, I didn't hear him. I had the last word.

I searched for Megan in the restaurant. I didn't see her because it was so crowded. I'd have to text her from outside.

The evening was cool. I was glad as it was refreshing. I was boiling inside. I texted Megan I was leaving. Megan texted me back.

Megan: What's going on?

Me: Justin's a jerk! Going home.

Megan: want me to come with u?

Me: not necessary.

Megan: u in the restaurant?

Me: out front.

Megan: coming out.

A few minutes later Megan appeared. "What happened?" she asked.

I gave her a summary.

"Wow. He's got some nerve," she said.

"Megan. I'm fine. Really. I don't want to ruin your evening."

I was affronted and angry, but not upset as if I had just broken up with someone. I really would be fine. I didn't want Megan's good time to come to an abrupt end.

"Only if you are really okay. Look me in the eye."

I looked her straight in the eye. "Yes. I'm really okay."

Megan knew I was telling the truth. "Okay," she said. "I really like this guy. His name is Zack. He's a lawyer."

"Have fun," I said.

"I will," replied Megan as we hugged.

I hailed a taxi and Megan headed back into *Renaud's*. At least one of us was having a nice evening.

On the taxi ride home I thought about Justin. Darn. Why did someone so handsome have to be such a jerk? And why was there still a part of me that was attracted to him?

CHAPTER 16

When I got home, I headed straight for my bedroom. I stripped down and walked to the bathroom for a shower. I needed to wash away the evening. While I was generally against getting involved with a client, I wasn't particularly bothered by the fact Justin had hit on me. What bothered me was *the way* he hit on me.

My time would probably be better spent figuring out how I was going to handle the account. Assuming, of course, Justin didn't fire us. No, he's not going to do that. He's too arrogant. He still expects I will go out with him.

I decided I would just be professional about the whole situation. I would do my work on the account and present it to Justin as I would any other client. No mention of the evening. If he brought it up, I would respectfully tell him all was forgotten and we could move on with the business of his advertising campaign. Period. The end.

I finished my shower and got ready for bed. I put on Old Navy boxer pajama shorts and slipped on a matching top. I slid between the cool sheets of my bed.

I wondered if Justin had picked someone else up. I bet he had. So why, exactly, am I even attracted to him?

Justin Renaud would be no good for me. He didn't deserve to be with me; not even for one date. But could he change? Maybe it was all an act to cover up some sort of insecurity. Maybe Justin was trying to protect himself in some weird way.

"Ugh!" I screamed out loud as I dropped back onto my pillow.

I stared up at the ceiling and thought of nothing and everything. I had a hard time understanding why I hadn't already let this go. I felt there was more to Justin. I needed to decide if it was worth trying to figure out.

I couldn't sleep so I decided to go to the living room and watch some television. I grabbed my phone from the bedside table. I often checked email and texts while I watched TV. Rachel Cooper, expert multi-tasker.

I plopped down on the couch and fished for the TV remote between the couch cushions. When I found it, I flipped through about twenty channels. I landed on an episode of *Friends*. I put down the remote and started checking work emails on my phone.

There was an unread email from Justin. Had I missed an email from him? Unlikely. I checked the date and time. He had sent it only twenty minutes earlier.

I tossed my phone to the side. *It's the weekend. You can check it on Monday*, I thought. I focused on *Friends*: The One with the Baby Shower. I wondered if I was named after Jennifer Aniston's character on the show. Probably not. My parents weren't in the Friends audience demographic.

Then I started to focus on having a baby. I wanted kids one day. Would I ever meet "Mr. Right" and get married? I was only twenty-four, though. No need to worry about that yet, right?

My problem, according to Megan, was an issue of being too picky. I thought Roger might turn out to be the guy for me. However, when he was offered a job in Dallas he decided I came second and was expendable. I had been on dates since then. I just hadn't met a guy that interested me enough. Maybe I was too picky.

I glanced at my iPhone sitting next to me on the couch. Nine unread emails. One of them was from Justin. An email from him within the past thirty minutes.

Against my better judgment I picked my phone back up. I scrolled to Justin's email. I tapped on the screen to open the message.

To: Rachel Cooper

From: Justin Renaud

Rachel,

I've been thinking about you. Have you been thinking about me? I know I came on strong. Nonetheless, I still think we both want the same thing. Don't you agree?

Justin

He was so arrogant. But was he wrong? Wrong for me, yes. But he wasn't wrong about my wanting to go on a date with him. How could I possibly be thinking about going on a date with such an arrogant jerk? But I was. Justin Renaud was going to be trouble for me.

CHAPTER 17

I was preparing breakfast when I heard Megan emerge from her bedroom. Megan came around the corner into the kitchen. She was wearing her New York Giants jersey that went down to her knees. Sports jerseys were her preferred sleeping apparel.

"I take it that it went well with Zack? At least I'm assuming it was Zack who walked you to the door last night?"

"Yes. Things went extremely well with Zack."

Megan poured herself a cup of coffee from the pot I had just made.

"You want some eggs?" I asked.

"Sounds great."

"Are you going to see him again?"

"Yes. We had a fun time last night. He's smart, funny, and very easy on the eyes."

"So Zack may last more than one or two dates?"

"Time will tell. But we are having dinner tonight and he invited me to the Knicks game Wednesday night."

"That's a start," I said.

I mixed the eggs and poured them into the heated pan. I scrambled as they firmed.

"Do you mind putting some bacon in the microwave?" I asked Megan.

"Do you want it extra crispy?"

"Yes. Please."

"I'm sorry your evening was a bust," said Megan.

"Thanks. I watched TV in the living room until I was ready to fall asleep."

"Were you thinking about what happened with Justin?"

"I hate to admit it. But, yes. On top of that he sent me an email last night."

"Really? What did it say?"

"Basically what he had said to me in person. He did admit he came on strong, but still insists I want to go out with him."

"At least he's consistent."

"That's what troubles me."

"I don't know why you would even give it a second thought. Unless . . . wait! You're not actually thinking about going out with him, are you?!"

"Not actively considering, no. But the thought is not far from my mind."

"So much for your business principles."

"He is all wrong for me. Yet . . ."

"You find him irresistible."

"Not irresistible. Alluring, perhaps. But it does bother me."

"Hmm. Alluring is a slippery slope toward irresistible. First you find him mysteriously attractive and next thing you know he is too attractive and tempting to be resisted."

I gave Megan a funny look. It's not that Megan isn't smart, but what she said was just too close to dictionary definitions.

"What? I had one of those word a day calendars. I guess a lot of the definitions stuck in my head. The interesting ones, anyway," she said.

"Do you think it is possible there is more to him than meets the eye?" I asked Megan.

One thing was for certain, Megan knew a lot about men. She probably knew enough to have a PhD in male behavioral psychology.

"Could be. He most certainly has commitment issues. I'd have to talk to him more to get a better read on him."

The microwave buzzed and Megan removed the bacon. It was sizzling and smelled wonderful. I finished scrambling the eggs and dished them onto our plates. Megan added the bacon strips and we made our way to the kitchen table.

"How dangerous would it be for me to go on one date with Justin?"

"Why do you even want to? I mean, beyond the obvious fact he is gorgeous? You said it yourself, he is all wrong for you."

"I know. And yet . . ."

"He is alluring," said Megan completing my statement.

"Which, as you have pointed out, would be a slippery slope to irresistible," I said.

"And you're in deep trouble if you reach irresistible?"

"I think so. I would want to try to build a relationship with him. A relationship, in all likelihood, he does not want. Not just with me, but with any woman."

"Sounds to me like that can only lead to bad things, Rache. Maybe you need to steer clear of this guy."

"Not possible. I'm managing the account, remember?"

"You could always hand the account off to someone else."

"Can't. Charlie basically told me this account is my ticket to bigger accounts and another promotion. Provided I do a good job. If I give it up, I will seriously stall my career."

"Given the circumstances, I'm sure Charlie would understand," said Megan.

"You may be right. But I don't want to take the chance. I don't want to put any doubt in his mind. Worse, I don't want him having to defend me to Mr. Sloane."

"Do you want me to go with you to your next meeting with Justin?"

"Maybe. Let me think about it."

I finished my bacon and eggs. I downed the rest of my orange juice.

"I'm going for a run," I said. "Maybe it will clear my head. You want to join me?"

"Another time. I need to get some work done on the Peterson account before dinner with Zack tonight."

"Okay. Thanks for the talk, Megs."

"Anytime. I'm always here for you."

"I know."

I gave Megan a quick hug. I picked up my plate.

"Just leave it," said Megan. "I'll take care of the dishes."

"You're the best," I said.

I padded toward my bedroom to put on my running clothes. I hoped a nice run through Central Park would release my tension and clear my mind. Maybe then I would be able gain the perspective I needed to deal with my situation with Justin.

CHAPTER 18

I put on a pair of black running shorts and a hot pink running shirt that said "Run" above the Nike swish logo. I laced up my new pair of running shoes and then headed out. It was a beautiful fall day. The air was cool. *Nice day for a run*, I thought.

I caught the subway to Central Park. The subway car was crowded. A few teenage boys took advantage of the close quarters and "accidentally" brushed their hands across my butt. I gave them a look that told them I knew what they were up to. I managed to make it the rest of the ride to Central Park without being fondled.

As I exited the subway station I could feel a gentle autumn breeze. The wind felt good against my body after being crammed on the subway car for fifteen minutes. I entered the park and stretched. I then started my run along one of the many paths that wind their way through the park.

Before long I was deep into the park. There were many people walking, running, biking, and rollerblading. But the path I ran on was not overly crowded. The leaves on the trees were just beginning to turn their autumn colors. I loved New York this time of year.

I picked up my pace as I wound through the center of the park. The wind rustled the leaves on the trees, birds were chirping, and squirrels were gathering nuts for the winter. It was easy to forget I was in the middle of New York City.

As I rounded a bend, I heard a familiar voice call out to me. "Rachel!"

It sure sounded like Justin. Aside from physical exercise, this run was to specifically clear my head of him. The last thing I expected, or needed, was to see him. *Ignore him. Just keep running.* I told myself.

"Rachel, hold up!" Justin called to me a second time.

I slowed my pace a little. There was no way to deny I heard him the second time. He was too close for me not to have heard him. We both knew it. Justin strode up beside me.

"Fancy seeing you here," he said between breaths.

"Yeah. What is up with that?" I said as I picked up my pace again.

He would either keep up or be left in my dust.

"What do you mean?" he asked as he kept stride with me.

"Oh, I don't know. There's, what, eight million people in New York City? Nearly two million in Manhattan alone. What are the odds we would meet each other on a random path in Central Park?"

"What are you suggesting, Rachel?"

I stopped on the side of the path. Justin stopped as well. He turned toward me.

"Are you stalking me?" I asked as I caught my breath.

"Rachel, I don't need to stalk women."

"That doesn't really answer my question."

"No. I am not stalking you. I run this exact path at this exact time nearly every single day. I live just off Central Park," he said, using our stopping point to catch his own breath.

"So it's just coincidence, then?"

If what he was saying were true about his running habits, then it was possible. I had never run this particular path before.

And I had no regular schedule for when I ran. I had no real way of knowing if Justin was telling the truth or not.

"Yes. A very nice coincidence," he said.

"That depends on your perspective," I replied.

"Ouch. That stings a little."

"Truth can sometimes hurt."

I was trying my hardest to reject Justin on any personal level. I knew deep down how much I wanted to go on a date with him. I was trying to keep that feeling buried very deep within me. I couldn't afford to let it come to the surface.

"I know you're sore from my behavior last night. I was much too forward with you."

"Yes. You were. And I have every right to be upset with you."

"Rachel. I know I can be a jerk. I've heard it before. But I very rarely get turned down. When I do, I always find someone else to say 'yes' to my flirtations."

"How nice for you."

"It is nice for me."

"Okay, I think we're done here," I said as I stepped back onto the path.

"Rachel, wait. I know how it sounds. But I'm not saying anything that isn't true. There are many women who will agree to go on a date with me. That is a fact. There are a small number of women who reject me. Also, a fact. But none of those women captivated me. I simply moved on. Found the next 'yes' after the rare 'no.'"

I stood with my hands on my hips. I don't know why I hadn't just resumed my run. My legs wanted to get moving again. But I was still standing there. Maybe this was a form of rubbernecking. It was bad but I couldn't keep from looking. Human curiosity.

"Just what are you trying to tell me?" I asked.

"You captivate me. You are different from the other women. I want to go out with you. I may even need to go out with you. I think you feel the same way about me."

I dropped my arms to my side and shook my head.

"No. That is where you are wrong. I don't need you. In fact, you are all wrong for me. We are wrong for each other."

"Okay. I can accept you don't need me. And I agree we are probably wrong for each other. What you didn't say is you don't want to go out with me. Need and want are not the same thing. Wanting to go out with me is enough."

"No. It isn't. Not for me," I said.

"Are you sure about that, Rachel?"

Justin took a step toward me. It wasn't threatening. But he intended to get into my personal space. I didn't move. I easily could have, but I stayed.

I began to speak but Justin stopped me by kissing me on the mouth. It was soft and gentle. He did have soft, yet masculine, lips. He tasted sweet.

"You can leave now if you want. I'll even run in the other direction," Justin said as he gazed into my eyes.

Why did he have to have such dreamy eyes? I shook my head. I knew I should leave. But I didn't want to. Was want trumping need? Was desire trumping sound judgment?

"Let me know where we go from here," Justin said.

I didn't respond. I didn't know how to respond. I wondered what to do next.

"Rachel, let me know what's next." Justin turned and began to jog down the path.

As I watched him round the corner, I didn't know for certain what was next. I only knew I was hooked. I needed to either make a clean break or take a chance that Mr. Wrong might turn out to be Mr. Right.

CHAPTER 19

"Rachel, let me know what's next." . . .

Justin's words from earlier in the morning kept ringing in my ears. It was all I could think about as I rode the subway home. It was on my mind as I rode the elevator in my building. I barely remember opening the door to my apartment.

"How was your run? Looks like a gorgeous fall day out there."

I snapped back into focus at the sound of Megan's voice. She was smiling at me from the kitchen table. Her laptop was open and papers were spread across the table.

"Fine. Yes, very nice out. I don't want to disturb you. I'm going to take a shower," I answered.

"Hold it right there," Megan said firmly. "Something's wrong. What happened? Are you okay?"

"I'm not sure I'm ready to talk about it."

"You didn't get mugged or attacked, did you?"

"No. Not exactly."

"What do you mean 'not exactly'? Rachel, you're scaring me. What happened?"

"I wasn't mugged or attacked. I did have an encounter though. I'm trying to figure out how I feel about it."

"Rache, just what the heck is going on? Who, or what, did you have an encounter with?"

Obviously Megan had blown right past the 'I'm not ready to talk about it' part. But she was genuinely concerned. As I would be for her. I decided now was as good a time as any to tell her what had happened.

"Okay, I'll tell you. But I need to sit down."

Megan and I sat on the couch. She had a look of real concern on her face. I patted her leg.

"It's not all that bad, Megs. I'm just a bit dazed and confused. I saw Justin while I was running in the park." I decided to start at the beginning and work toward the rest.

"Did he see you? I mean, I'm assuming he was your encounter?"

"Yes. He actually saw me first. I was running ahead of him."

"Was he stalking you? Should we call the police?"

"No. I don't think he was stalking me. He claims he runs the exact path at the exact time practically every day. I suppose it could be true."

"I suppose. But, still . . ."

"I know. Look, I'm not worried about that so much. I take him at his word. There are times when I have randomly bumped into someone I know. It does happen, even in a city as large as New York."

"I guess." Megan didn't sound too convinced.

"He told me he doesn't need to stalk women. And why would he? We both know he has no trouble getting dates. So let's move on from the whole 'Justin was stalking Rachel' line of thinking. Okay?"

"Okay. As long as you believe him."

"I do."

"Alright. What happened next?"

"He told me he had come on strong last night. He knew he could be a jerk."

"Both true," Megan said.

"He also told me how much he wanted to go out with me. That he needs me."

"Okay. So he's still angling to get you to go on a date."

"More than that. He told me he is captivated by me. That I am different from other women. Even the small number of women who reject him."

"Oh my gosh! Rache, did you seriously fall for that baloney?!"

"Megs, you weren't there. I am fully aware what a guy will say to get you to go out with him. But there was something in the way he said everything. His body language. I don't know . . ."

"I do know. You've lost your mind. Rachel, Justin Renaud is a player. He is playing you. Don't read anything more into it than that."

Normally I would agree with Megan. She is far more adept at male behavior than I am. But I wasn't ready to accept Justin was as shallow as he appeared. I felt there was something more going on. Even if Justin didn't want to admit it, or even realized it yet.

"I think there is more to Justin than being a player," I said.

"Rachel, this is what happens when you try to see traits in a guy that aren't actually there. You are trying to convince yourself Justin is Mr. Right."

"I don't think I am trying to make Justin out to be something simply because I want him to be the right guy. I really think there is more to him than what he projects on the surface."

"I think you're delusional. He is all wrong for you, Rache. You know it. I know it. He probably knows it. Let me fix you up with somebody. I promise he will be super nice and really cute. I can help you find the real Mr. Right."

Megan was pleading with me because she saw me slipping toward an infatuation with Justin. She knew what happened when I became fixated on something. I knew she feared I would end up being used and tossed aside.

"Hold the phone," I finally said. "I think I can decide who I want to date."

"So now you want to date Justin?"

"I don't know. I'm trying to sort this all out. I was confused about Justin when I got up this morning. I'm only more confused now."

"Rache, please listen to me. Justin is bad news for you."

"And you get to decide that?"

"He moves at a different speed from you. He wants something entirely different from what you are looking for. He isn't right for you."

"I've heard enough. Thanks for the talk." I jumped up from the couch and headed toward my room.

"Don't be mad at me, Rachel. I'm just worried about you."

Megan may have been right. She probably was right. But I was mad. I wanted her to tell me to "go for it" or "give it a chance and see where it goes." She didn't come close to either of those. I have no idea why I thought she would.

"I just need some time to think about this," I said.

I would think about it more. But I was pretty sure what my decision was going to be. Talking with Megan had the opposite effect than I suspected it would. I wanted to find out if there was more to Justin Renaud. I was ready to take a chance Mr. Wrong might turn out to be Mr. Right.

CHAPTER 20

Justin

I ran the same path in Central Park at the same time almost every day. It was my time to myself. I had been a runner since high school. I ran to help stay in shape.

It was a nice surprise seeing Rachel jogging ahead of me. Maybe it was fate. Maybe just dumb luck. Whatever it was I seized the moment. Carpe Diem.

I hadn't planned on it happening. Not exactly the way it did. I knew I wanted to talk to her. Despite what she said to me last night, I knew Rachel would want to talk to me as well.

I've never needed a woman before. Not like this. What scared me was I might give in. I wanted Rachel Cooper that much. I might need her and it would change what I was willing to do to be with her.

I didn't like it. But perhaps I didn't have a choice. Not if I wanted to be with Rachel. I could choose to walk away. But I didn't think I would.

I looked at myself in the mirror. "What is happening?" I asked myself out loud.

I stripped off my running clothes. I started the water in the shower and stepped in. I didn't wait for the water to warm. I needed a cold shower.

Maybe a cold shower would snap some sense into me. In the end, it turned out just to be a cold shower.

I toweled off and headed to my bedroom to get dressed. I was meeting Nick at the restaurant to go over our liquor order. That was what I needed – to focus on work. Work led my mind to our advertising campaign with Jacobs & Sloane.

Why did Charlie Jacobs have to assign Rachel Cooper to my account? He said she was a very promising junior executive. I had Charlie to blame for all of this. I didn't know whether I would one day thank him or want to throttle him.

"Rachel, let me know what's next."

That was the last thing that I had said to her in the park. I knew she was going to let me know. I suspected she wanted to explore going out with with me.

The question was how far I was willing to take things with her? Could I see myself past one date? Could a second date lead to a third?

I don't do relationships. Could I reconsider that position for Rachel? Would I have to? Time would tell.

The fact I would even think about it scared me. Rachel was trouble for me. A trouble I was already willing to consider accepting.

CHAPTER 21

Rachel

When I reemerged from showering and changing, Megan paid no attention to me. She was engrossed in her work and must have figured there was nothing left to say at that point. I really wasn't mad at her. How could I be when she was just trying to be a good friend.

"Megs, I'm sorry. I know you are just looking out for me," I said as I stood in front of the kitchen table.

"I know. I just don't want this to end in a horrible mess. You giving yourself fully to this guy and him tossing you aside when he's decided you've served your purpose."

"It's a risk I'm willing to take. I'm going in with my eyes wide open."

"You sure about that?"

"Maybe I need to take a few more risks to find the elusive relationship. To find my Prince Charming. I believe a very wise woman once said I should be a little less picky and take a chance."

"I knew it would come back to bite me in the butt."

"I'll let you get back to work. I'm going to do a little clothes shopping and then pick up some groceries. You need anything at the grocery store?"

"We could use some more apples. Red Delicious if they look good and are on sale."

"You got it."

I grabbed my purse and headed for the subway. Fortunately I found a seat and settled in. Macy's was having a fall sale and I wanted to pick up a few outfits. A few fetching outfits. I was going all in with taking a chance with Justin.

I put in my ear buds and scrolled through my music files. I selected some Maroon 5. I loved Adam Levine's songwriting and his falsetto voice. He was also easy on the eyes.

I scrolled through my email. I was secretly hoping there would be another message from Justin. I don't know why I thought he would email me again, but I checked anyway. Nothing.

Should I contact him? I thought.

He did kinda leave the ball in my court: *"Rachel, let me know what's next."*

I could email him. I could also text him. I had his business card in my Renaud's file. I knew his cell number was on it. I texted Megan and asked her to get the file from my bedroom. She texted back.

Megan: Got it.
Me: Justin's cell number?
Megan: Ugh...don't make me
Me: Number please.
Megan: 212-555-4378
Me: Thx!
Megan: whatever

Okay, Megan was less than thrilled I was going to contact Justin. But at least I had his cellphone number. Now, what was I going to say?

Me: Want to discuss what's next...

I waited a few moments. Then my text message tone dinged.

Justin: Free tonight?
Me: Maybe. What do you have in mind?
Justin: Dinner?
Me: Where?
Justin: Is that a 'yes'?
Me: Yes, unless I don't like the restaurant :-)
Justin: cute. How about Bouley's?
Me: Fancy. Yes.
Justin: pick u up at 7?
Me: I'll meet you there 7:30
Justin: OK. See you at Bouley's 7:30.
Me: see ya then

Bouley was a French restaurant in the Tribeca neighborhood. I'd heard great things about it. The food and atmosphere would be wonderful. I hoped our conversation wold be as well. Bouley wold also be neutral territory.

Had I taken a risk in texting Justin already? Did I seem anxious? Or, worse, desperate? Maybe. But he responded right away. He wanted to see me tonight.

I felt a little more in control of the situation. I took a deep breath and relaxed a little.

I arrived at the 34th Street Herald Square stop and exited the subway. I made my way to street level and then continued the 300 or so feet to Macy's on 34th Street. As I entered the store I made my way to the 3rd floor. I headed straight for the Women's Clothing department.

"Can I help you find something in particular?" asked the sales associate as I flipped through a dress rack. Her name tag told me she was Estelle.

"Actually, yes. I'm looking for a fall dress for a dinner date. Above the knee but I want to cover my chest," I said.

"Ah, something that is flirty but doesn't give anything away?" said Estelle.

"Exactly."

"I have a few dresses that I think you will like."

Estelle led me over to the Guess display. She gave me three good choices to try on. We both agreed that the Mock-Turtleneck Lace-Overlay Illusion Dress was my best choice.

The dress was just what I was hoping to find. Sophisticated and flirty with only the slightest hint of cleavage behind the black lace print that covered the top. It was long sleeve, so perfect for an autumn evening in New York.

The dress hit at the thigh. That way I could show off most of my legs. I was striking just the right balance of being fetching without "giving it away" as Estelle had stated. I also got it for under $100, so I was happy.

Estelle rang me up and I headed out of Macy's before I had the chance to do any more damage to my credit card. I decided on a shorter trip to the grocery store. I wanted time to get the dress cleaned before I met Justin for dinner.

Megan was just finishing her work when I got home. I told her about dinner and modeled the dress for her. She grudgingly agreed dinner at Bouley's would be fabulous and I was a knock out in the dress. If it had been anyone other than Justin, she would have been totally giddy.

Megan had softened a bit as the rest of the afternoon wore on. She and I helped each other get ready for our respective dates. We gave each other a final look over. Zack picked Megan up for their dinner and I headed out to meet Justin. Dinner would tell me a lot about whether taking this step was a good idea or not.

CHAPTER 22

Justin was waiting for me out front of Bouley's when I arrived at seven-thirty. He looked dashing in a pair of black slacks, light gray wool blazer, a crisp white shirt, and a light gray tie with charcoal and black stripes. He smelled divine.

He smiled as I approached. I knew he liked the way I looked in my new dress.

"You look absolutely beautiful," he said as I walked up to him. He took my hand and kissed it.

"You don't look half bad yourself," I said with a sly smile of my own.

"Shall we?" he said as he extended his hand toward me. I took him by the hand and we walked toward the front door. He opened the door and let me enter first. *So far, so good*, I thought. *But it's early yet.*

Bouley was beautiful. The walls were light in color and had large impressionistic paintings on them. There was an arched ceiling and square, white columns dotted the far wall. In the center of that wall was a small wood fireplace.

The tables were elegantly decorated with fine table cloths and candlelight. We were seated at a table for two near the fireplace. The low back cushion chairs were decorated in a lovely pattern. Justin ordered a bottle of Champagne as we looked over the menu.

After the waiter poured our champagne, Justin raised his glass. I raised mine as well.

"To whatever is next," he said.

"I suppose I can drink to that," I said.

We toasted and took a sip from our glasses. The champagne was wonderful. I made certain to pace myself. I needed to stay in control.

The waiter returned a few moments later take our order. For an appetizer, I ordered Porcini Flan and Justin had Chilled Wellfleet Oysters. I decided on Wild Alaskan Salmon for my entree and Justin ordered the Dry Aged New York Sirloin.

"So, what is next Rachel?" Justin asked after the waiter finished taking our order.

"Appetizers. Then dinner. I'm hoping for stimulating conversation and for you to sweep me off my feet. After that . . . We'll just have to see."

"That's a lot more than I typically have to invest," he replied.

"And yet here you are," I said as I tilted my glass in his direction before I took a sip.

"Yes. Here I am."

I wasn't sure if Justin was expertly playing me or I had truly gained the upper hand. I decided I was going to continue to play as though I did have the upper hand. If I stuck to it long enough, eventually I would have it by default.

"You don't think very much of me, do you?" he asked.

"That depends. You are a successful businessman at a young age. You seem quite smart. You are devilishly handsome. On the surface there is quite a bit to be impressed with."

"I feel a 'but' coming on," he commented.

"Then you open your mouth and say things that cause me to give pause. You show hubris. In other areas, it would be attractive. In matters of women and relationships, it is anything but attractive."

"And yet here we are. Having dinner together."

I needed to be careful. I didn't want Justin to gain control of the conversation. I needed to know more about him.

"We are. But this is to discover what's next beyond dinner. Beyond tonight."

"And if dinner goes well?" he asked.

I smiled at him. I was stalling. I was trying to think of what to say next. I think he knew it as well.

Justin smiled back at me. He was patient. He took a sip of his champagne. Our appetizers arrived. It bought me another moment.

"This looks wonderful," I said.

"It does. But you still haven't answered my question."

"No. I haven't."

"And you're not going to?"

"I don't believe I need to."

"No. You don't."

We finished our appetizers in relative silence. When our entrees arrived, I decided to shift the focus of our conversation. I gave up on Justin romancing me and sweeping me off my feet. It didn't seem to come naturally to him. Eventually he would have to make an effort at it.

Maybe I could get him to reveal a little more about himself. Perhaps I could begin to understand why he acted the way he did. I still felt he had layers to be peeled back. I remembered from my psychology classes in college that family of origin could explain a lot about a person.

It was certainly true of me. I grew up in a middle class family in New England. My parents were the first in their families to go to college. They valued education and life experiences. I was the oldest of three children. My sister was three years younger and my brother was five years younger than me.

I experienced all the firsts of my siblings. My parents were overly cautious with me and also overly joyous with my accomplishments. My sister exhibited a lot of middle child tendencies. My brother was still the baby of the family.

All of that aside, I grew up in a loving and supportive household. My parents still had a happy marriage. I looked at the life they had built for themselves and it was the life I wanted someday.

I suspected Justin was either rebelling against a similar upbringing or had a very different type of experience from mine. There was only way to begin to learn more about him. I needed to ask. I doubted he would openly volunteer any information.

"When we met to go over your account, you mentioned your ancestors migrating to Quebec from France and then your grandparents coming here from Quebec. Tell me more about your family."

"Not much to tell. My grandfather was a very accomplished pastry chef."

"You had already mentioned that. You also mentioned you have brothers. What was it like growing up for you guys?"

"Does any of that really matter?"

"I'm just trying to get to know you better."

"I don't hear you talking about your family," he said rather abruptly.

I clearly hit a nerve. Justin definitely did not want to talk about his family. Fine. I'd talk about mine. I told him about my parents, my brother and sister, and what it was like growing up in Newton, Massachusetts.

"Did you know the Fig Newton is named after my hometown?"

"I didn't," Justin replied. "It sounds like you had a great childhood. A nice family. That explains a lot."

"What's that supposed to mean?"

"We are all products of our environments, to one degree or another. You seem to have it mostly together. You know what you are looking for in a relationship. In life. You're not willing to settle for less."

"And why should I?"

"I didn't say you should. But you may not find any of that with me. I don't know if I am capable of thinking in those terms."

I wasn't expecting such brute honesty from Justin. At least not in that way. Not when it came to feelings or relationships. But it was a thread to pull on. I just wondered if I should pull. Would it be too much?

I decided that we probably had hit an end point in this particular conversation. We had more of a conversation than we ever had before. I considered it progress. Maybe it was best to leave it where it was at for the night. The best I could do was put the ball in his court.

"So what's next Justin?"

CHAPTER 23

Justin downed the remainder of the champagne in his glass. He sat back in his chair and stared at me.

"I don't think there is a next," he said after a few minutes. "I was right about you, Rachel. I knew you'd be trouble for me."

"Trouble? How am I trouble for you? I would think it would be the other way around."

"What I mean is I am content with the way I live my life. There is a calm and peace to it. It's uncomplicated. My desire to be with you disrupts that."

"I've never seen myself as being disruptive," I said.

"No. I don't suppose you would. Rachel, your impression of me after last night was correct. I'm afraid there really is nothing more to me."

"What? My impression you were an arrogant jerk? That impression?"

Justin grinned. We were slipping backwards to where we were last night at *Renaud's*.

"I wasn't thinking exactly of those little terms of endearment, but you are not off the mark."

"So that is who you are? Straight up . . . There is absolutely nothing more to you?"

"Pretty much. Like I said, Rachel, I keep things pretty uncomplicated."

"So I complicate things for you?"

"I suppose you could say that, yes."

"Why are we even here then?"

"Look, I thought maybe . . ." Justin's voice trailed off and he looked away.

"Maybe, what?" I asked.

"Maybe you would be worth the trouble. Maybe I would be willing to have my life complicated to see if there was anything between us."

"Then what you are saying is I am not worth it?"

"Not exactly."

"I get this date isn't going so well. I get we are opposites in almost every way. I even get we're probably wrong for each other. But I'd like a better explanation than what you are giving me. Just saying I am 'sort of not worth it' doesn't cut it for me."

"Rachel, I don't do flowers and chocolate. I don't engage in stimulating conversation and sweep women off their feet. Not in the romantic, wonderful date sort of way you think of. I don't do romance. I don't date. The fact I am even here having dinner with you was a major concession for me."

I let what Justin was saying sink in for a moment. Could I have been so wrong about him? Was there really nothing more to him? Did I have to accept I was attracted to a man who had no depth to his character?

"I'm not sure what to say," I said. And I didn't. I was at a loss for words.

"I'm not sure there is really anything to be said. It is what it is. It doesn't change the fact I am captivated by you. It was enough for me to come on a date with you. It was enough for me to consider the possibility I would offer more to be with you . . ."

"But you won't . . . offer more?"

"No. I just can't. I think we both need to admit this little experiment isn't working."

"Experiment?"

"Yes. You wanted to discover if there was more to me, if I could offer you more. I wanted to see if I could offer more, assuming I had to. Obviously it is a non-starter."

"It sounds a bit crass when you put it that way," I said.

Justin simply shrugged his shoulders. Not dismissive of my comment, but in recognition it was simply how he saw the situation. It was rather uncomplicated for him. I struggled as I found it more complex.

"Rachel, you want the flowers and chocolate and all the other stuff. You want commitment. You want a relationship. I can't give you those things."

I nodded my head. He was at least admitting that there was no chance he would ever offer them to me.

"Despite the fact I can be an arrogant jerk, I'm not going to pretend I can give you those things when I can't. You deserve better than that."

"You're right. I'm not. I guess I can appreciate your honesty. But this wasn't just some 'little experiment' to me. I did hope for more. I'm sorry it didn't work out."

It was the best that I could come up with. To be honest, I'm not sure there was much else I could have said. Justin hadn't been completely wrong in what he had said. I knew this had been a gamble, but it still felt bad. It never feels good to have a date go down the tubes.

Justin paid the check and we left. I thanked him for dinner. The evening hadn't been a total loss. The food and ambiance of Bouley's was magnificent. I also took comfort in how much everyone else at the restaurant were enjoying the company they were with.

"I can speak with Charlie Jacobs about reassigning your account," I offered as Justin and I stood on the sidewalk.

"That won't be necessary. You are doing a great job. I want you on the account. I see no reason we can't maintain a professional relationship. Unless it presents a problem for you?"

"No. Not at all. Of course we can," I replied.

"Fine. Let me know when you have more of the campaign for me to look at."

A taxi pulled up and Justin opened the back door for me. I got in.

"I'll get the next one," he told me as he closed the door. "Good night."

"Good night," I replied. I gave the driver my address and we pulled away.

I glanced back at Justin standing on the sidewalk. It was perfectly clear there was never going to be anything between us. Justin didn't do relationships. But I still felt he was avoiding being completely honest with me. Almost as if he were afraid. But afraid of what?

CHAPTER 24

Justin

I stood alone on the sidewalk as Rachel pulled away in the taxi. I was just being honest with her. The very act of having dinner with her came dangerously close to a normal date. I thought I could handle it. I wanted to try.

In the end, I realized I am not ready to complicate my life. Not even for Rachel Cooper. But it was hard. Rachel looked amazing. And if I ever could be in a relationship, Rachel would be the person I would want to be in it with.

A second taxi pulled up in front of the restaurant. I hopped in. I thought about stopping by *Renaud's*. No, I was sure my assistant manager had everything under control. I would hear otherwise.

"Where to buddy?" the taxi driver asked me.

I gave him my home address. I needed to stay away from the restaurant tonight. I looked out the window of the taxi as the city lights flickered past. *You were honest with Rachel,* I thought. *So why do you feel so bad. Why haven't you already let this go? Why are you still thinking about her?*

"Good question," I said aloud.

"What?" asked the driver.

"Sorry. Nothing. Just thinking out loud."

"They say that's a sign of intelligence," replied the driver.

I didn't feel so smart. I knew how my life was and what I had said to Rachel. But, I had to admit, I was conflicted.

I pushed Rachel away. Pretty definitively, I might add. Was it necessary? Should I have let it play out a little longer?

My cellphone buzzed in my pocket. I pulled it out and checked the display. It was the restaurant.

"Yeah?" I answered.

"Justin, it's Nick. Sam doesn't look so great. I think he's got the flu."

Sam was my assistant manager. I certainly didn't want him at the restaurant if he was sick.

"Tell him to go home. I'll be there in a few." I hung up.

"Change of plans," I announced to the driver. "Take me to Renaud's, please." I gave him the address.

The driver altered our route and we arrived at the restaurant ten minutes later. Business looked as good tonight as it had been since we opened. I paid the driver and approached the front door.

Tank, who worked security, nodded at me. His nickname fit. His given name was Gerald, but no one ever called him Gerald. I think even his mother called him Tank.

"Sam sounded like he was coughing up a lung," Tank said to me.

"I heard. He go home?" I said.

"I put him in a taxi about five minutes ago."

"Good. I'll call him later to see how he is doing."

I moved past Tank and into the restaurant. I stopped by the bar to let Nick know I had arrived.

"Sam looked like terrible," he said to me.

"Tank put him in a taxi home," I replied. "Business good tonight?"

"It's been great. Might be our best night yet," he answered.

"I should take a night off more often," I said.

"Oh, yeah. Sorry to call you while you were out with Rachel."

Nick glanced around. "She with you?"

"No. Didn't go so well," I said.

"Too bad. But, hey, plenty of fish in the sea," Nick said with a wink.

"Get back to work," I said.

Nick gave a nod and went back to filling drink orders. I turned around and surveyed the room. It had been hard work opening the restaurant, but I was thrilled with how well we were doing.

Maybe we didn't need the Jacobs & Sloane advertising campaign. I quickly pushed the thought out of my head. I knew it was more about avoiding Rachel than the fact a good campaign would bring in even more business. Maybe even enough for a second location. Plus, the whole reason for hiring Jacobs & Sloane was to get the right image for *Renaud's*.

I went to my office and closed the door. I picked up a tennis ball and bounced it off the wall. I couldn't stop thinking about Rachel. She got through a chink in my armor. A suit of armor I had spent my entire life putting on.

There was a brief moment where I almost opened completely up to Rachel. Part of me wanted to tell her about my parents horrible marriage. About all their arguing and how I would hide under my bed and cover my ears to try to block it out and pretend it wasn't happening.

I almost let Rachel see inside my head and my heart. I came close to trusting her enough to open up about my life. Almost. I caught the tennis ball and squeezed it in my hand.

Despite my insistence to the contrary at dinner, my life was more compromised and complicated than I cared to admit. Rachel Cooper had taken a hold of me. *Okay, what is next Justin?* I asked myself.

CHAPTER 25

I sat behind my desk and called Andrew. He picked up on the third ring. It was noisy in the background.

"Hey, little bro," he yelled into his phone.

"Where are you?" I asked.

"Delaney's Pub. Watching the Yankees game," he answered.

"You have time after the game?"

"For my little brother? Of course. What's going on?"

"I just want to talk to you about something."

"Sounds serious."

"Might be. Might be temporary insanity. Not sure which. Hopefully you can help me figure it out."

"Where are you now?"

"My office at the restaurant."

"I'll be there in twenty minutes."

"Don't rush."

"It's okay. Yankees are behind and it doesn't look like they will catch up. I'm leaving now."

"Thanks. See you in twenty."

"See ya."

Delaney's Pub was Drew's favorite place to watch the Yankees, Giants, and Knicks. He loved their Irish ale. Delaney's was at most a fifteen minute taxi ride from *Renaud's*. If Drew caught a taxi right away, he could be in my office from his bar stool in the twenty minutes, give or take a few minutes.

Twenty-three minutes later, Drew was sitting on the couch in my office. He had taken an extra minute or two to grab a bottle of beer from Nick at the bar. He took a pull on his beer and sat back on the couch.

"So, what is going on?" he asked me.

"I think I must be coming down with something."

"Like what?"

"Not sure. All I know is that I had dinner with this one woman and I think she is getting to me."

"Back up a little. You actually had dinner with a woman? Like a real date?"

"Sort of."

"What do you mean? Was it a date or not?"

"In theory, yes. But not a good one."

"Well, seeing as how you don't really date . . ."

"It's not that. It was bad because I actually tried to have a normal dinner date. But I ended up giving her the standard disclaimer how I don't do romance, commitment, or any of that."

"Okay. I get that part. What I am confused about is why you asked a woman out on a date to begin with. That's out of character for you bro. Who is this chick?"

"Rachel Cooper. The advertising exec handling the restaurant's account."

"She must be something."

"She is. At least I think she is. Enough to take her to dinner."

"Justin, there has to be more to this story."

"There is."

"Are you going to share?"

"I almost opened up to her."

"Oh, the horror," teased Andrew.

"Very funny."

"Sorry. I couldn't resist. So you like her? I mean, like a normal guy might like a normal girl?"

"Maybe. I don't know. But she intrigues me. There is something about her. I can't put my finger on it. Why am I reacting so differently to her?"

"Rachel and Justin sitting in a tree . . ."

"Shut up! What are you ten years old? I'm trying to be serious here."

"Sorry, again. Look, it sounds to me like you have some feelings for this Rachel. I know it is scary territory for you. I mean mom and dad had a bad marriage. What we all lived through is enough to make us swear off relationships. But, Justin, it's not like we have some gene from dad that is going to automatically make us fail at a relationship."

"So why aren't any of us in a relationship?"

"If you asked the question several months ago you know I could tell you Matthew almost proposed to Kathleen and I was six months into dating Barbara. Neither of those worked out for us. But, Justin, we do date. It looks like David may be heading toward a relationship with the woman he has been seeing recently."

"Victoria," said Justin.

Andrew nodded and took another tug at his beer. "She's very nice. She might even be the one for David."

"Okay, so I'm the only screwed up brother?"

"I didn't say that. But you are the youngest. You were a pretty young kid during some of mom and dad's worst fights. You hadn't even experienced dating. You were still in your 'girls are icky' phase. I just think it impacted you differently. Harder."

"What, like I'm scarred or something?"

"I'm a lawyer, not a psychologist. But I'd say it definitely did something to you it didn't to Matt, Dave, and me. Not that we aren't more cautious, and maybe even more skeptical about marriage, but we are not opposed to it. And we've had some pretty good and healthy relationships."

I just sat for a minute and thought about what Drew was saying. I guess it made some sense. Maybe it explained my aversion to commitment and relationships.

"Let me ask you this," continued Andrew. "Do you in any way want to see Rachel beyond a casual date? Do you think you might want to explore having a relationship with her?"

"I don't know. But I'm willing to consider it is a possibility. I actually regret how the conversation turned out between us," I replied.

"For you, that is a pretty big deal."

"Perhaps," I said. We both knew there was more. I didn't want to freak myself out by saying it.

Andrew nodded his head. He took another sip of his beer. Then he leaned forward on the couch and looked at me.

"Maybe you are ready to wrestle with some stuff and make a commitment."

"That would be pretty deep," I said.

"It would be. Welcome to being a well-adjusted adult."

"I wouldn't go that far," I said.

"Yeah, me neither. But it is a step in the right direction. Think how happy mom will be to know her baby might turn out fairly normal after all."

"Ha ha, very funny."

"So what are you going to do?"

"I guess I'll call her. I don't know after that."

"It's a start." Andrew stood up and patted me on the shoulder. "I'm always around when you need to talk."

"I know. Thanks."

"Let me know what happens," Drew said as he headed toward my office door.

"I will," I said. "Oh, and Drew?"

"Yeah?"

"Don't say anything to Dave or Matt. And especially not Mom. I don't know where this is going, if anywhere. I just don't want to get into it with them right now."

"Understood. Good talk, Justin."

Andrew headed out of my office and closed the door. I didn't know how right Andrew was. I was afraid he was more right than wrong about this.

The big question was whether or not I was capable of taking the next step. Thinking I might want to take the step and actually taking it were two entirely different things. How successful I was at this depended on how badly I wanted it. How badly I wanted to explore a relationship with Rachel Cooper.

CHAPTER 26

Rachel

The apartment was empty when I got home. I'd have it to myself for the evening. Megan had texted she was going out with Zack. At least one of us was having a good time.

I tossed my purse on the table by the front door and kicked my shoes off. I headed for the kitchen to put on the kettle. I figured a cup of hot cocoa was in order. I thought of ice cream, but eating ice cream alone after a bad date seemed too depressing.

I opened the pantry and grabbed a bag of microwave popcorn. I decided that I'd look for a movie on Netflix. Hot cocoa, popcorn, and a movie. I guess I could get with that program. Not that I had many other options.

I placed the bag in the microwave and hit the popcorn button. I stood and waited for the water to boil for my instant hot cocoa. I remembered my mother telling me that a watched pot never boils. Same idea.

As I thought about it, it didn't actually make any sense. Of course it boiled if you watched. If it had water and the stove was on, the water in the pot, or kettle, was going to boil whether you watched it or not. It just seemed to take less time if you weren't standing there waiting for it. I guess that was the point to the saying.

If ever there was a sign that I needed to make some changes in my life, that could have been it. I was twenty-five years old, living in Manhattan, and it was Saturday night. What was I doing? Reflecting on the saying of a "watched pot never boils." Seriously?

To be fair, though, I did have a date earlier. It just didn't go so well. But it was probably doomed to fail from the get go. I still needed to make some changes.

Tonight Megan was out again with Zack. She'd been on more dates the past six months than I'd been on the past three years.

I realized the kettle was whistling. I tore open a hot cocoa package and poured it into a mug. I poured the hot water and stirred. The microwave had also beeped. I got a bowl for the popcorn.

Just another crazy night for Rachel Cooper in the Big Apple. I left the cocoa and popcorn on the living room table and went to my room to get out of my dress. As I headed down the hall, I heard my cellphone ring.

I went for my purse and pulled my phone out. 212-555-4378. I recognized the number from this morning. It was Justin.

"Hello," I said as I answered.

"Rachel. It's Justin. I needed to talk to you. Actually, I need to see you."

"Well, I just got home. My date was kind of a bust."

"Mine didn't go so well either. Of course it was on me. I'd really like to see you tonight."

"Did you find another way to tell me you have commitment issues?"

"I'm sorry about earlier. Can I see you to talk?"

"Not if you are just playing games or you are going to toy with my emotions."

"No games. I don't want to play with your emotions. But we need to talk. Despite what I said at dinner, I can't shake the thought of you. I can't leave things the way they are right now."

"Okay. We can talk. I'll meet you at Starbucks," I said. I gave him the address of the Starbucks near my apartment.

"Okay. I'll see you in a half hour," he said.

"See you then."

We hung up. What just happened? My heart was racing. My palms were sweaty.

I went to my bedroom to change. I decided to wear jeans and a sweater. I didn't want to be in the same clothes I had worn to dinner. For some reason it seemed sad. Like I was mourning a hopeful date that was dead on arrival.

Of course that was silly. I told him I had just gotten home. It was perfectly reasonable I would still be dressed from dinner. I was over thinking it.

I still decided on a pair of navy blue jeans and a mint sweater. I was going to give the appearance of this being totally casual. No remnants of our failed date from earlier in the evening. *Let's see how this goes*, I thought to myself.

CHAPTER 27

I arrived at the Starbucks around the corner from my apartment building ten minutes before Justin and I were to meet. Since I didn't get to drink my hot cocoa at the apartment I ordered one there. I found a table near the back. I sat so I could watch the door for Justin.

I removed the lid on the cup to let the hot chocolate cool a little. I wrapped my hands around the cup. The warmth felt good on my hands. It had turned out to be a rather cool fall evening. The sweater and jeans turned out to be a smart choice.

Justin arrived five minutes later. He spotted me and walked over to the table. He was wearing a pair of dark jeans and a light gray sweater. Now I was really glad that I had selected jeans and a sweater.

"I'm going to grab a snack. Can I get you anything?" he said when he arrived at the table.

"No, thank you. I'm good with the hot chocolate."

"Be right back."

I watched Justin as he went to the counter and pointed at a cookie in the display case and put in a drink order. He came back a few minutes later with a chocolate chip cookie and a hot chocolate with extra whipped cream.

"I wouldn't have taken you for hot chocolate," I said as he sat.

"My mom made it for us all the time when it was cold outside. Habit, I guess."

He broke off a piece of his cookie. "Sure you don't want some?"

The cookie looked good. I was tempted. But I didn't have much of an appetite. My nerves had really kicked in.

"No. Thanks," I replied.

Justin popped the piece of cookie in his mouth. He seemed cool and collected. So far we were treating this like it was a normal get together. Just two friends meeting at Starbucks. Maybe neither one of us had really thought this through.

"Thank you for agreeing to see me," Justin said after he had finished his piece of cookie.

"Well, you did pique my interest. I guess curiosity got the best of me. Hopefully, I don't suffer the same fate as the poor cat in the saying," I said.

Justin thought for a second. Then he nodded.

"There is nothing about this that should be lethal in any way," Justin said with a grin. "Except maybe for me."

"How so?" I asked.

"My evening is already far more compromised and complicated than I have ever allowed an evening to become. That happened before I even called you. Seeing you again is a whole other level. I'm really flying without a net here. I'm just hoping not to plummet to my death."

"So we both recognize we are taking a big risk being here together," I observed.

"And probably for the same reason. But from a different perspective."

"Can we quit with the metaphors and speak directly? You were very direct with me at dinner, so I know you have it in you."

"Okay. You're right. I owe you a direct explanation as to why I called and wanted to see you. Needed to see you."

"Needed?"

"Yes. Hadn't I mentioned that on the phone?"

"Perhaps you did."

For the first time I sensed that Justin was vulnerable. Not just vulnerable, but he knew he was vulnerable. He was even tipping his hand to me he was. I was sticking with my wait and see attitude.

"I didn't handle dinner well. What I said was true. It was how I felt. Or how I thought I felt. It was certainly the way I have always felt up until this evening."

Justin took a sip of his hot chocolate. I think he was buying some time to consider his next words. Then again, we were in a Starbucks and had yummy hot chocolate to drink. I decided it was a little of both.

"And what changed?" I asked. "About the way you have felt up until this evening?"

"You. I don't know why. I just know it's you."

"It's me, what?"

"It's just you. Look, I'm not a psychologist. Heck, I'm not even experienced in dating and having feelings about someone. Seeing women casually? That I know. Relationships? Not a clue."

"Are you saying you want to explore a relationship with me? After emphatically telling me you don't do relationships?"

"Rachel, in all honesty, I don't know what I am telling you. I just know I feel different about you. I can't stop thinking about you."

"It's nice to know you have been thinking of me. But, that alone, does not make you prime dating material."

"I know everything about my attitude toward relationships is wrong for you. But can I get a little credit for even having this conversation?"

Truth be told, I was somewhat impressed with Justin. Given where he was coming from, he was making an effort. But I wasn't going to let him off for dinner that easily.

"You're right. You do deserve a little credit. It still doesn't exactly make you ready to commit to a normal dating life. Much less a normal relationship."

"I get it. You have every reason to be skeptical. To be honest, I don't know if I can do it. I didn't even think I would be able to call you this evening. You would be taking a huge risk on me."

"Can I ask you something?"

"Sure."

"Just why are you so afraid of any sort of commitment. Of a relationship of any kind?"

"Easy. At least according to my brother Drew. My parents."

"Bad marriage?"

"That's a major understatement. They had a terrible marriage. They argued every minute of every day they were together. I don't know how they ever got along. Let alone loved each other."

"They must have once. I mean, they got married. They had kids."

"I suppose."

"But your memories are all of a terrible marriage?"

"I don't remember a happy time between them. My dad left seven years ago. The divorce was bitter. I swore I would never get married. The only way to protect against the possibility was to never have a relationship."

"I'm sorry. I didn't know any of that."

"I hadn't told you before now. I've never shared this with any woman."

"Even that would have been too much of a commitment? Getting too close to a relationship?"

"Yes."

"From a psychological standpoint I think it sort of makes sense."

"Now you sound like Drew."

"You've talked to him about this?"

"Yeah. Earlier tonight. Just before I called you. Drew is the one person I have always been able to talk to."

"It's nice to have someone you can talk to."

"Yeah. He's my oldest brother. He's always looked out for me. He tried to protect me from my parents fighting when I was little. But it's hard to protect somebody from something when it is constant."

"So, Drew helped you see something about what happened between us at dinner? Or what was going on with what you might be feeling?"

Justin shuddered a bit. "I don't do feelings well. But, in a manner of speaking, yeah. Drew helped me see some stuff."

"Okay. What sort of stuff did Drew help you see?"

"I don't see you like all other women. There is something more about what I might be willing to consider with you."

I didn't think Justin was playing me. When he talked about his parents there was genuine pain there. He clearly had a mistrust of relationships from his experience growing up with parents who despised each other. Worse, they didn't, or couldn't, hide their troubles from their children.

I was beginning to think Justin was emotionally scarred and his commitment issues were a form of putting up defenses. He also thought enough about what had happened between us to talk to his older brother about it.

Okay, he had some serious baggage. But, in a strange way, it made wanting to be with him more real. At least there was a reasonable explanation for why he behaved as he did. There was even a willingness on his part to explore it. Or so it seemed to me.

"That explains a lot, actually. And I truly feel bad your view of marriage, and relationships in general, has been shaped but such a negative experience. I still don't know what to make of where it leaves things with us. You have a lot you would need to deal with to have a healthy relationship."

"What? Like therapy?"

"Probably wouldn't hurt. There is nothing wrong with seeing a therapist."

"I bet Drew would agree with you. I probably do have a lot of stuff to deal with."

I nodded. It was tough to argue with him on that one. Did Justin really want to turn a corner and move forward?

"I think I like Drew," I said with a grin.

"Drew is a pretty awesome brother."

I was seeing more of who Justin was in this conversation. He had brothers, or at least one of his brothers, he had a solid relationship with. He seemed close to Drew. Even looked up to him. It seemed Justin could be honest and vulnerable with him. He was even showing some vulnerability with me.

"So, what does any of this mean?" Justin asked.

"I think there are issues you need to work through. With a professional. But it doesn't mean we can't talk about next steps."

I meant it. If Justin wanted to make a real effort, I certainly was willing to take a chance with him.

"So, do I get another chance at dinner? To get a date right?"

"Yes."

Justin smiled and sipped his hot chocolate. I did the same.

CHAPTER 28

The sun streamed through my bedroom window as I rolled over and blinked my eyes open. I was still amazed at the turn of events. Somehow I had gone from a terrible dinner date to a possible relationship with Justin.

I put on my robe and headed to the kitchen to start a pot of coffee. The apartment was quiet. Megan was still sleeping. I added the coffee grinds, poured the water into the machine, and placed the pot in position for the coffee to brew.

I received an incoming text message. I glanced at the screen. Roger.

> *Roger: Hey Rachel. How have u been? I'm moving back to NYC. I miss u like crazy. I was stupid to take a promotion in Dallas over staying with you. It may be too late for us, but I hope not. I'd love to see you. Maybe we can talk about picking up where we left off? Or start over? At least get together and discuss it? I hope you will say 'yes' to at least getting together.*

I sat stunned as I stared at Roger's message. I honestly didn't know what to think. Why was I not immediately dismissing Roger's message? Why hadn't I already tapped out a polite reply telling him I had moved on?

Even if it didn't work out with Justin, it had been more than a year since Roger and I broke up. Did I still hold a torch for him?

I was startled as my phone rang in my hand. Justin was calling.

"Hello," I said answering.

"Hi, Rachel. I was wondering if you would like to get together for brunch?"

"Um, okay," I said blankly.

"Everything okay?" asked Justin.

"Oh, um, yes. Sorry, just spacing out I guess. Everything is fine," I replied.

But everything was not fine. I was ready to take a chance with Justin. But Roger's text had me questioning my decision. Could Justin be a mistake?

I wondered if I should get out before it went any further. Would I still be with Roger if he hadn't left? Did I still want a relationship with him after more than a year and over 1,500 miles between us?

The timing on Roger's message was terrible. Or was it? I thought I was beginning to find answers with Justin. Now all I had were questions.

Now what's next, I muttered to myself. I had no idea.

CHAPTER 29

I was able to focus enough to make it through brunch with Justin. If he suspected something was wrong, he didn't let on. Despite a major step forward with Justin, Roger's text had thrown me for a loop.

Justin dropped me off at my building. We shared a nice kiss in the taxi before I hopped out. He was meeting his brothers for a Knicks game at Madison Square Garden. I was relieved he had plans. I needed some time to think.

Megan was out with Zack again. I had texted her my plans and she replied she'd be home about a half hour after me.

When I got to my apartment, I plopped down on the couch. I opened my message from Roger. I read the text over and over. I became fixated on what I was taking as key parts of his message.

I'm moving back to NYC.

I miss u like crazy.

Maybe we can talk about picking up where we left off?

Or start over?

I hadn't replied yet. I knew I needed to. Even if I responded with a polite 'no,' I figured it would be inconsiderate to ignore him.

Granted, he chose to effectively leave me when he accepted his promotion in Dallas. But I was the one who wasn't ready to live together or consider a move to stay together. Neither seemed unreasonable of me at the time.

Still not unreasonable, I thought. I liked Roger a lot. He was, is, a great guy. I could have seen a future with him. Could

I still consider the possibility of a future with him? Was that possibility greater than what I might find with Justin?

"Ugh!" I let out a grunt of frustration.

I heard a key in the lock and then Megan opened the door.

"Hey, Rache," she called as she entered our apartment.

"You are not going to believe the twenty-four hours that I've had," I said.

"Do tell," Megan said as she flopped on the couch next to me.

"How about something to drink?" I asked.

"Sure."

"Let's sit at the kitchen table," I offered.

"Um, okay," said Megan, looking a little perplexed.

I poured us each a glass of juice and we sat at the kitchen table.

"Okay," Megan said after we were seated. "What happened?"

"Actually, no. Dinner was a complete bust. Not the meal itself. Bouley's is incredible. But the conversation part. The date ended at dinner."

"So how did you go from that to dating Justin?"

"Let me finish," I said. "He called me and was very apologetic. He had been doing some thinking and had a heart-to-heart with his oldest brother. He practically begged me to meet him to talk. I agreed. We had a very revealing conversation at Starbucks. It was enough to convince me to take a chance."

"What, exactly, did he say?"

"His parents had a crappy marriage. A worse than crappy marriage. Justin's lifestyle has been a defense against having a bad relationship. He at least gets that part of it now."

"Whoa. Rache, this guy has some serious commitment and relationship issues. I get he is handsome, successful, and can be charming, but do you think it is worth the risk you are taking with him? I mean, and I can't believe I am saying this, but he might have too much baggage."

"I'm fully aware. Believe me, I considered everything. But a combination of his vulnerability, honesty got to me."

"So you think you can be the one to save this guy from himself? Turn him from a commitment-phobe into a family man?"

"I wouldn't put it quite that way," I said.

"Hmm . . . ," was all Megan said in reply.

"But it is only half of it," I said.

"Am I going need to something stronger than juice?" asked Megan.

"Maybe we both will," I said. "I got a text from Roger earlier today. Just after I had talked to you."

I pulled up the text message and showed it to Megan. She read it and then sat back in her chair. She let out a sigh.

"So what are you thinking?" Megan asked.

"I'm thinking I don't know if Justin could end up being the right guy or if this is another chance to be with Roger. A guy who is great and I could have easily seen myself with long-term. And maybe I can still see myself with Roger. But I am also drawn to Justin. I want him to be able to commit to me and see where it takes us."

"Okay, that statement just made my head spin," said Megan.

"Welcome to my world," I responded.

"Did you text Roger back?"

"Not yet."

"But you're going to?"

"Yes. I just don't know what to tell him."

"Do you want to get together with him? See what comes of it?"

"I don't know. What about Justin?"

"Look, you had a three plus month relationship with Roger. Yes, he accepted a job in Dallas and you two broke up. But it sure seems like he regrets the decision. I always liked Roger. Justin I'm not so sure about."

"I get what you are saying. And part of me agrees with you. The other part feels like I've made this commitment to walking down a road of discovery with Justin. Wouldn't I just be dropping him like a hot potato?"

"Maybe. I don't know. Rache, you need to do what is best for you. You are not Justin's savior, Rachel. If he really wants to make this change then he will. He should want to do it for himself."

"What if he is doing it because of me? What if I am the reason he wants to change?"

"Again, you are not responsible for his actions. Only he is. Yes, maybe he is doing it because he wants to be with you and this is the only way. But is that enough for the long- term? If it isn't what he really wants for himself, then it won't last. He'll just break your heart and Roger will end up with someone else."

"My head hurts," I said as I grabbed my forehead. "This literally has given me a headache."

"There's some aspirin in the cabinet," said Megan. "But you need to think long and hard about this. Do you think Justin could be the guy for you? I mean deep down? Or is this the chance to get back with someone you already saw as a very good contender as the guy for you? Roger made a stupid decision leaving you. Looks like he now knows it now. I think it should count for something."

"Okay. It seems pretty clear where you come down on this," I said.

"Perhaps. But what I think doesn't really matter in the end. You have to make the decision that is best for you. The decision that is going to make *you* happy."

"The problem is I have no clue what that is going to be."

"I didn't say it would be easy. And I'm here for you."

I nodded my head. Megan was a great friend. I was lucky to have her in my life.

"I think I at least need to find out more about when Roger is moving back. Then I'll take it from there."

"It's a start."

I got my phone off the living room coffee table and called Roger.

CHAPTER 30

I sat on my bed as I pulled Roger up in my contacts list. I paused for a moment and then hit the call button. I waited as the phone rang. I thought about ending the call, but Roger would only see that I tried to call and didn't leave a message.

My heart was racing. I didn't know why I was so nervous. I'd spoken with Roger hundreds of times on the phone. I'd spent countless hours with him over three months. He and I had slept together many times.

Of course it had been over a year since we broke up and he moved to Dallas. It had been almost a year since we had last spoken. A few emails, texts, and Facebook comments had been the extent of our communication since then. On the third ring, Roger answered.

"Hi, Rachel," he said. He was out of breath. "I was packing in the other room and had to run to find my phone."

"Already packing? So is moving day getting close?"

It was the best opening line I could think of. Seemed appropriate enough. A bit of beating around the bush, but it was a start.

"Two weeks. I'm packing nights and weekends. I take it you got my text?"

Roger seemed pretty relaxed. Maybe he was confident that I would want to get back together. Maybe he was as nervous as I was but really good at hiding it. I wasn't sure which.

"I did. Sorry it took me a little time to get back to you. I had brunch with a friend today. This is my first opportunity . . ."

"Don't worry about it. I wasn't expecting to hear from you right away. I know I kinda threw it out there. I thought of calling, but I figured a text you could ignore until you were ready to respond."

"Roger, I don't know what to say right now. It was really hard when you left. I'm going to need some time to think. And what happened with your girlfriend in Dallas?"

There was silence on the other end of the phone for a moment.

"She was very nice. I liked her a lot. But . . . she wasn't you. Rachel, I realized that I made a mistake leaving."

"So you just broke up with her and decided to move back to New York?"

"Sort of. I knew Rebecca wasn't going to be long-term. Maybe she turned out to be a rebound relationship. I don't know. All I know is I was constantly comparing her to you."

Roger paused a moment to see if I had anything to say. I didn't at that moment. He continued.

"My job here in Dallas is great. I like the work and the staff I manage. But the Data Analytics field is really growing right now. I have options. My company's growth has been tremendous this past year. There are even positions equivalent to mine in Manhattan now."

"So you asked for a transfer back to New York?"

"Yes. We need more managers for the Northeast region. They could transfer me or lose me to another company. They opted to transfer me back. I know the Manhattan office well and they saw my moving back as an asset."

"And you are doing all of this in hopes of our getting back together again?"

"It's a major reason. But you know I have a lot of friends in New York and my family is in Pennsylvania. There are a lot of reasons this makes sense for me."

"So did you decided to come back and then figure 'what the heck, why don't I see if Rachel is still available'?"

"It's not like that, Rachel."

"Sounds a little like that. It sounds like your decision to move to Dallas in reverse. Dallas was a good move for you and I became dispensable in that decision. Now moving back to New York is good for you. Suddenly I am convenient again."

"That's not totally true, Rachel, and you know it. Yes, the move to Dallas made sense for my career at the time. Yes, I had made the decision without first discussing it with you. But I also wanted you to consider a move to Dallas. So, okay, I didn't handle the situation well. And, yes, I have already decided to move back to Manhattan. And you may not want to get back together, but why is it wrong for me to want to explore the possibility you might?"

"I guess it's not. But what would prevent you from making another major decision, say to move somewhere else, without first discussing it with me? And let's assume I said I didn't want to move? Would you still go again?"

"That's a lot of what ifs?"

"But not unreasonable given the situation."

"Okay. Fair enough. Rachel, I won't make the same mistake twice. If we get back together then I'm not ever going anywhere without you again. If a hypothetical move isn't what we both want, then I wouldn't be going anywhere."

"I'm still going to need more time to think about all of this. Things are a little more complicated than just deciding whether or not I want to get back together with you."

"Are you dating someone else?"

"It has been over a year, Roger. I sort of am. I don't know. That's part of what is complicated."

"Doesn't sound too serious."

"Roger, how would you know what it is or isn't?"

"I don't, really. I'm just saying you don't sound very clear on whether or not you are actually dating somebody. To me, that doesn't sound very serious."

"Roger, I just need some time."

"So you have said."

"I'll talk to you later."

"Okay. Talk to you later."

Roger then ended our call. I was glad I had at least responded to his text. I was, however, no less confused about what I was going to do.

CHAPTER 31

Justin

Maybe Andrew was right. Maybe I was ready to deal with my commitment issues and make an actual attempt at a relationship. But could I actually go through with? Could I stick with one woman?

I didn't know. I would be tested. I guessed I would start to find out the answer when temptation was staring me in the face. I had already taken a pretty big step in treating my evening with Rachel differently than I had with any other woman.

Rachel certainly knew that. She knew we were entering uncharted waters. For both of us. Maybe with the light of day Rachel was having second thoughts. She seemed a bit distracted at brunch.

Was it the phone message she received? I thought to myself. Her disposition seemed to change after. Am I actually analyzing this relationship? Can I even call this a relationship?

It would have to wait. The taxi pulled up to Madison Square Garden. I paid the driver and hopped out. I texted Drew to tell him I had arrived. He messaged back that they were waiting for me outside the Tower A entrance.

I found Drew, Dave, and Matt and we made our way to our seats. Dave had scored us seats in the 100 level at center court.

"How did you get such great seats?" I asked David.

"A client has seasons tickets. He couldn't make the game tonight and offered them to me. I've made him a ton of money for retirement. I guess he wanted to show his appreciation."

Dave was a financial planner. He was very good at what he did. Each of my brothers were successful in their careers. Andrew was an attorney and Matthew managed one of New York's top hotels. While I never said it, it was one of the reasons that I wanted Renaud's to do so well. I wanted to measure up to the success my brothers had.

We took our seats in time for the Knicks warm-up. It had been a while since I had attended a game. I loved basketball. All four of the Renaud boys did. Probably the one positive thing our dad shared with us.

The Knicks have won the NBA championship twice. Both long before I was born. My dad was a teenager when they won it all in the early 1970's. The last time they made the finals was 1989, the year I was born, when they lost to the San Antonio Spurs. But we were ever hopeful.

"So what do you think our chances are this year?" I asked.

"Of what? An NBA title?" asked Dave.

"Yeah," I replied. Guess I was an eternal basketball optimist.

My brothers all laughed.

"We can always hope," said Matt.

I was seated next to Drew on the end of our row. Matt was adjacent to Drew while Dave sat on the other side of Matt. I was glad because our seating arrangement would give me a chance to talk a little with Drew during the game. Matt and Dave would get so absorbed in the action on the court they wouldn't notice our conversation. Besides, it would be too loud in the arena for them to make out what we were saying unless we spoke up enough for them to hear.

As the game got started, Drew leaned toward me.

"So, did you call Rachel?"

"More than that."

Drew raised his eyebrows and looked at me.

"Do tell, little bro," he said, with keen interest.

"We got together at a Starbucks and had a positive conversation. We then had brunch the next day."

"Big step for you," he stated.

"Yeah. Pretty huge," I agreed.

"So what's next?"

"I don't know. I'm thinking you may have been right."

"About having a normal relationship with a woman?"

"Yeah. I mean, I don't know if that is what is happening. But . . ."

"But you're thinking about it?"

"Yes. I think Rachel might be worth trying to figure out if I can actually make the commitment."

"I've got to meet the girl who can do this to you," said Drew with a smile.

"Hold your horses. I know I am not ready for her to meet any of the family. I probably have miles to go."

"Okay. I'll hold off on setting up the family dinner."

"Do you think I will need help doing this?"

"What kind of help?"

"Professional help?"

"What? Like a shrink?"

"Rachel said I could probably benefit from seeing a therapist about commitment issues. You know, work out my stuff about mom and dad."

Andrew sat back and thought for a moment. He took a sip of his beer. Andrew liked to drink beer when he thought. I wondered how he made decisions at work without a cold lager in his hand.

"Maybe," he finally said.

"All I get is a 'maybe' out of you?"

"I suppose it couldn't hurt to go once. See if it helps."

"You don't sound entirely convinced," I said.

"Mom got Dad to see a marriage counselor once. Didn't do them any good," Andrew replied.

"I think Mom and Dad were beyond help."

"True," Andrew agreed. "Dad didn't even try. As long as you are open to it, why not? Give it a go."

"Maybe I will."

"Rachel really has a hold on you, doesn't she?"

"Strange, isn't it?"

"Strange. But good. At least I think so."

I nodded. I had a lot to think about. We enjoyed the rest of the game and then went out for pizza. Andrew was a rock in my life. David and Matthew didn't always see eye to eye with me, especially over opening Renaud's, but I knew they had my back.

After dinner, I headed home. I thought about stopping by the restaurant, but it would be a slow evening.

I also wanted to see Rachel again. *You are in uncharted waters, Justin Renaud*, I thought to myself. I smiled. It was a nervous smile, but a smile nonetheless.

CHAPTER 32

Rachel

"Shake a leg, Cooper, we're going to be late!" shouted Megan from the front door.

I had overslept and was rushing to get ready for work.

"I'm coming!" I replied as I dashed down the hall.

I pulled my jacket on and slung my purse over my shoulder.

"Sorry, Megs. I had trouble getting to sleep last night. My mind kept racing."

"The Justin or Roger debate?"

"Yes," I said as I closed our door behind us.

Megan was already at the elevator and had punched the button.

"Don't you have a meeting with Justin today?"

"Yes. A lunch meeting."

"What are you going to say to him?"

"I still don't know. I'm hoping to delay it as long as possible. It is, after all, a business meeting."

"Hmm. Do you recall what happened at your last business meeting?" asked Megan as the elevator arrived and we stepped on.

The doors closed and the elevator jerked downward.

"Very funny," I replied. "We have a lot of ground to cover on the campaign. I'm not leaving much time for anything else."

"That's your plan?"

"I know he will say something. Maybe want to set our next date. I guess I can at least handle that much."

"So you still think there may be something there with Justin? You're not at all concerned about his track record?"

"If I wasn't concerned, I would probably have already told Roger I've started to date someone else. But being concerned and calling it completely off before we really get started . . . I don't know if I can do that. Not just yet, anyway."

"What did you tell Roger?"

"That I needed to think about things."

"Deep."

"Why are you so snarky this morning?"

"Sorry. I guess I need to just let you figure this out."

"You know I value your opinion, Megs. This is just very confusing for me. I'm really torn about this."

"I know you are. I'm sorry. I just don't want to see you get hurt."

"Well, there is a chance of that no matter what I decide."

"I guess that is true."

We reached the lobby. Mrs. Shwartz and her Yorkie, Grace, were waiting for the elevator.

"Good morning, Mrs. Shwartz," I said.

"Oh, hello, dear. Say, that was a real hunk I saw you with the other day." Mrs. Shwartz attempted a wink.

"Have a nice day, Mrs. Shwartz," I said as Megan and I crossed the lobby.

"Hunk?" Megan said. "Who says that anymore?"

"Megs, she's like eighty years old. I'm impressed she came up with *hunk* instead of *dreamboat* or something like that."

Megan and I giggled as we stepped out into the cool autumn air.

"I don't think we have time for the subway," said Megan as she glanced at her watch.

"It's my fault. I'll pay for a taxi," I said.

I wasn't convinced we would get there much faster in rush hour traffic, but a taxi probably did give us the best chance to arrive to work on time. At least we could go door to door and not have to navigate the stairs and crowds on the train.

Megan stood near the curb and made sure her legs and bust were clearly visible as she hailed for a taxi.

"What decade are we in?" I asked.

A taxi pulled up moments later. Megan gave me a little smile as we piled into the back.

We arrived in front of our office building with five minutes to spare. When we reached our floor, we dashed to our offices to deposit our coats and purses. We each grabbed our coffee mugs and met back in the conference room just in time for the Monday morning staff meeting. The coffee carafe made its way around the table. I filled my mug.

Ah, like sweet nectar, I thought as I took my first sip of the day. I settled into my chair as Charlie Jacobs began to speak.

"I have some very exciting news," beamed Charlie as he sat at the head of the conference table.

"I just learned Justin Renaud is doubling the budget for the Renaud's account. We should all congratulate Rachel for doing such an outstanding job on her first lead account."

I nearly choked on my coffee. What? Why was this the first I was hearing about this? As my colleagues applauded, Megan leaned over and whispered in my ear.

"Did Justin mention this to you?"

I shook my head no.

"Interesting," said Megan.

"In light of this good fortune," Charlie continued when the applause ended, "We will need to devote additional staff to the Renaud's account. Rachel, we can meet later this afternoon and discuss your staffing needs."

I simply nodded. I was still in a bit of shock. Doubling the campaign was a huge deal. I was at a loss as to why Justin wouldn't have said something to me about it. Unless he just decided to do it. Did he sense something was wrong? Was this a way to ensure that we spent more time together?

Even though we were only a few hours away from our lunch meeting, as soon as the staff meeting was over I headed to my office to call Justin. I wanted an explanation. I should be ecstatic at having the budget for my account doubled. But I was peeved at finding out this way. This development seemed a rather last-minute decision on Justin's part. I wanted to know why.

"Hi, Rachel," said Justin when he answered the phone.

"What is going on with doubling the account budget?"

"Whoa, hold on there. Why are you so upset? I figured you would be thrilled."

"I am. Or I normally would be. I just want to know why. It seems awfully sudden. You said nothing about this to me over the weekend."

"I just decided this morning. I called Charlie early to let him know."

"And you didn't think to let me know?"

"I texted you. Before I called Charlie, in fact."

I dug my cellphone out of my purse. Sure enough, there was a text from Justin. He told me he had discussed this with his brothers over dinner after the Knicks game and decided to expand the campaign. And he would be calling Charlie to let him know.

"Okay. Sorry. I overslept and Megan and I were rushing out of the apartment. I obviously didn't see your message in all the commotion."

"Obviously," he said.

It sounded like he was smiling on the other end of the phone. I don't know how you sense that someone is smiling over the phone, but I felt it.

"Did it just come up at dinner? You weren't thinking about it before then?"

"I was kicking it around. But I didn't want to say anything to you until I discussed it with my brothers. It's my decision to make, but I wanted their input. Especially Dave because he's the numbers guy. It was late when I got home last night and I didn't want to disturb you."

I relaxed my shoulders and eased into my chair behind my desk.

"Well, that makes sense. But doubling the campaign is a big commitment."

"If I didn't know better, I would think that you were trying to talk me out of spending more money with your company."

"No. Not at all. I just don't want you doing this because of, you know . . ."

"Don't worry about that. My brothers all thought it was a good idea. We want maximum exposure for the restaurant. Only Drew knows anything about us, so Matt and Dave's opinions are purely from a business perspective. If anything, Drew would have played devil's advocate if he thought I was motivated by anything other than the restaurant's business."

"That makes me feel better. Sorry. I guess I overreacted a little."

"No problem. And I am aware of the additional commitment I am making. It's the right move for the restaurant."

"Okay, then." I said.

"Besides, I'm not totally adverse to commitment."

Okay. I didn't think that Justin's last comment had anything to do with the Renaud's account with Jacobs & Sloane.

"See you at noon."

"I'll be there," Justin said.

We hung up and I tilted back in my chair. As if I wasn't confused enough. Justin was certainly making it harder on me. My cellphone dinged with a text message.

> *Roger: I know you are at work. Just hope you're not mad about our conversation the other day.*

> *Me: No. Just need . . . I almost said 'some time'. I'm not mad.*

> *Roger: Good. Talk later :-)*

> *Me: k*

Darn. Really not what I needed at the moment. I tossed my phone onto my desk. Charlie stopped by my office.

"Three o'clock good to meet?"

"That will be great, Charlie."

"Great. See you then. You're doing a super job kiddo," he said with a smile as he headed down the hall.

I had an hour before lunch with Justin. I actually did have some work to do before then. Justin vs. Roger would have to wait.

CHAPTER 33

I arrived at the restaurant five minutes before noon. Justin was waiting by the host station. I guess neither of us thought of how we would greet each other. Justin broke our awkward moment by kissing me on the cheek.

We were seated at a table by the window. People hustled by on the sidewalk outside. Busy New Yorkers on the way to lunch, meetings, and running errands. The waiter took our drink order and we looked over the menu.

I settled on a Grilled Chicken Caesar Salad. Justin went for Pasta with Alfredo Sauce. After we ordered, Justin clasped his hands and looked at me with a smile.

"What?" I asked as I looked back at him.

"Would it be inappropriate for me to tell you how great you look?"

"Well, I think you just did. So . . ."

"Right. I think for the first time in my life I am not exactly sure of what I am going to say to a woman. I know this is a business meeting to go over the account. But I think we blew past this just being about business Saturday night."

"Yes. But, Justin, I really need for us to stay focused on your campaign at lunch. I have a mountain of work at the office and a meeting with Charlie Jacobs this afternoon."

"Okay. I get it. All business today."

"Thank you."

"You're welcome. What are you doing after work?"

"I . . . I don't know."

"How about dinner? Something light. I really want to see you."

So much for avoiding a personal discussion. I wasn't sure about dinner.

"I don't know what time I'll be finished at work. I have a ton to do."

"Wow, a mountain and a ton. That's a lot of work."

"Don't be snide. I really do have a lot of work to get done this week."

"No problem. I get it. You have a busy *week*."

"Wait a second. Are you a little jealous? Of my work taking up my time?"

"No. I just thought if you had some time we could go out to dinner."

"I think you are jealous. Good for you. That says something about where you are with this."

"Okay. Guilty as charged. Believe me, this is a totally new feeling for me."

"Given the circumstances, it's cute."

"Great. That's exactly what I was going for."

"Oh, don't be touchy," I teased. "It's another step toward being in a normal relationship. Just be careful not to get too needy. That is a turnoff."

"Duly noted. However, I don't think my being needy is likely to be a problem."

"Yeah. Probably not. I'll let you know how my week is shaping up. For dinner one evening."

"I'll take it. Now, show me what you've got for the campaign."

Our lunch arrived and I spent the better part of an hour going over every aspect of our campaign. I got feedback from Justin on exactly how he wanted to expand based on the doubling of his budget. We had a productive meeting. There was also some flirting between us.

I don't think either of us intended it. It was just there. I had brushed against Justin's hand and excitement surged through my body. *Oh boy*.

"It all looks great. Very impressive," said Justin when I finished going over the specs for the advertising campaign.

"Thanks. I'll have a better idea about our expanded team after I meet with Charlie this afternoon."

Despite this being a business lunch, I also couldn't deny that we were personally connecting. It seemed like another step forward for us. Did this mean a step back in considering Roger? I didn't know. In the moment, I didn't care.

CHAPTER 34

Justin

I sat on the edge of my couch as I put my shoes on. My hand was shaking. All of a sudden I felt like I might pass out. I grabbed a bottle of water from my coffee table. I drank half the bottle.

I felt my pulse. It was returning to normal. My hand had stopped shaking. What was that?

"Sounds to me like you had a little panic attack," said Drew over the phone.

"A panic attack? I'm twenty-five and in excellent shape," I said.

"It has nothing to do with your age and what shape you are in," said Drew. "You are falling big time for Rachel and I think it's messing with you a little. Maybe you really should talk to a professional."

"Drew, I think I really like her. But I'm worried I won't be able to do this. You know, stick with it and have a . . ."

"Relationship," said Drew.

"Yeah. That."

"Justin, make an appointment to talk to somebody."

"So what? Do I just Google 'shrinks'?"

"I'm not sure you'd get anybody decent if you searched that way. 'Therapist,' 'Psychologist,' would give you better luck. But let me ask around. I'll find somebody for you to go see."

"Thanks, bro," I said.

"You got it. Hey, Justin?"

"Yeah?"

"I have got to meet Rachel."

"Let me make sure I can stick with her first. I wouldn't want to subject her to the rest of the Renaud boys unnecessarily."

"Fair enough. I'll call you later."

As I hung up I was positive I was in deep. *What are you doing to me Rachel Cooper?*

CHAPTER 35

Rachel

I somehow managed to get through my meeting with Charlie. I filled him on my meeting with Justin, minus the extra curricular activities, of course. He told me that he wanted to add another team member to the Renaud's account. He asked me for my input. We agreed on a recent hire from the creative group.

After my meeting with Charlie, I locked myself in my office for another hour to return phone calls and respond to some of the more urgent emails from the afternoon. I still had work to do, but I decided to come in early in the morning rather than stay late. At five thirty, I wandered down the hall to Megan's office.

She was staring at her computer monitor when I walked into her office and sat in the chair opposite her desk.

"You going to be able to get out of here?" I asked her.

"I probably should stay another half hour or so. But I could be persuaded to leave now."

I looked over my shoulder to make sure that no one was in the hall outside Megan's office. I leaned forward and whispered just to be on the safe side.

"How about cocktails and I tell you about what happened with Justin following our lunch meeting?"

"Give me five minutes," replied Megan.

Megan finished a memo she was working on for her account and then we hit a cocktail bar not far from our office. As soon as we purchased our drinks at the bar and settled into a table, Megan leaned forward anxiously.

"Okay, what happened?" she asked.

"Justin and I flirted over lunch."

"Does it mean you have made a decision?"

"I'm still not a hundred percent sure. I want to believe Justin will commit and see this through. I think I would regret not finding out."

"Justin does have serious commitment issues. Rachel, to be honest, I don't know how long any one woman could hold his attention before his natural instinct to flee kicks in."

"Other than he is making a real effort."

"Despite my reservations on the subject, it sounds to me like you are trying to convince yourself to try a relationship with Justin," concluded Megan.

"So do I dive into the deep end with him?" I asked.

"If you are ready to swim in those waters. I still think there is less risk in the shallow end with Roger. Even with his leaving once. But I think you are already jumping off the diving board."

"Okay, enough with the metaphor. I get it. Roger is probably the smart choice. The safe choice. The choice my head should make. But I feel my heart telling me something else. Even if it is a greater risk to my heart getting broken."

"There's your answer," said Megan.

"I suppose I should call Roger," I said.

"Yeah. I don't think you can approach starting a relationship half-way."

"All or nothing," I said.

"All or nothing."

"I'll call Roger tonight."

We finished our drinks and headed home. Megan and I changed into our lounging around outfits and fixed dinner. After we ate, I took a deep breath and went to my room to call Roger. I wasn't exactly sure of what I would say, but I felt that I was making the best decision for where I was in my life.

CHAPTER 36

I sat nervously on my bed as the phone rang. Roger answered on the third ring.

"Hi, Rachel," he answered in an upbeat, hopeful tone.

"Hi, Roger," I said. My tone was flat.

I'm not sure I consciously did it to counter Roger's cheeriness. It was probably more of just how I was feeling. I didn't want to give a false expectation.

"You don't sound very happy."

"I'm not happy nor am I unhappy. This is . . . just a difficult call for me to make."

"Oh. I guess I should assume it's not the news I was hoping to hear?" His voice had deflated from when he answered the phone.

"I'm sorry, Roger. I just think it has been too long a time for us. Yes, I know it's only fourteen months. But it's been fourteen months without you in my life. Fourteen months after you chose a job and a new city over me. Over . . . us."

"I already admitted that was a huge mistake and one I regret. I'm moving back to make it right," Roger protested.

"You said there were other reasons for why the move made sense. So, are you really coming back just in the hopes of getting back together with me?"

There was a long pause on the phone. I gave Roger a few moments to collect his thoughts, but I wasn't going to give him all night. He had to know the answer to the question.

"Basically, yes," he finally replied. "It is true what I told you about my work and being back with New York friends and closer to my family in Pennsylvania. But, yes, the move back was motivated by trying to get back with you."

"Roger, how could you make such a big decision without any information about my status? Without knowing how I felt about it?"

I was more convinced I had made the correct decision. Justin may have his issues, but he was looking to address them to be with me. Roger also had some pretty big issues. Ones I wasn't sure he was even aware of. Issues I was just beginning to see.

"I didn't think. I just want to be with you. I thought . . . I thought if I came back it could be like it was. Maybe even better."

"You should have talked to me before you made such a decision, Roger. I was right. This is just like your decision to move to Dallas. You figured in your mind how it should play out and based your decision on that. Not on the actual reality of the situation."

"You're right. I never thought about it," Roger said rather dejectedly.

"There's the problem, Roger. You didn't think about it. You didn't think about it fourteen months ago and you didn't think about it whenever you decided to make the move back. I don't want to be harsh, but it's pretty clear what is going on."

"Yes. You're right, okay?! I get it now! I've screwed up! I screwed up leaving and I've screwed up coming back!"

Whoa. Roger had turned on a dime. He was agitated. It actually scared me a little. I was glad we were on the phone and not in the same room.

"Roger, I didn't mean it quite like that. Nobody's perfect. We all make mistakes. All I am saying is that I don't know how much of an 'us' there really was. There can't be a true relationship when one person independently, without discussion, makes major decisions which impact the other. It was also a big assumption I would even still be available. I know I'm not a dating machine, but it has been over a year, after all."

"Alright. I get it! We are not going to happen again. I hope you are happy with your new boyfriend."

Roger's voice was edgy and sarcastic at best. There was a whole other side to Roger I had never witnessed before. It wasn't remotely endearing.

"Roger, please don't let this be how we end the call. I didn't want this to be confrontational. I don't want bitter feelings."

"I messed up. Twice. I'm mad at myself. All I wanted was another chance with you."

Roger was trying to recover composure, but he had a desperate tone.

"I am sorry, Roger. I know I told you I needed time to think. And I have given it a lot of thought. I have decided it is best for me to move on. I think you should do the same."

More silence on the phone. After a moment Roger spoke.

"I guess I don't have any other choice. You've made up your mind. Have a nice life."

Roger ended the call. It didn't go nearly as well as I had hoped. I figured Roger would be disappointed, but I didn't expect the reaction that I got. He seemed a little unhinged over the whole thing. Much more so than he certainly should have been after fourteen months.

I went into the living room where Megan was watching TV. She muted the volume when I came in and sat down on the couch.

"How did it go?" she asked.

"Not well. I'm a little worried about Roger. He seemed to take it especially hard. I actually thought he seemed rather irrational. He scared me a little."

I recapped the conversation with Megan. When I finished, she shook her head.

"Yeah, I would tend to agree with you. Seems like he overreacted. Maybe Roger has a few screws loose we just didn't see before."

"Could be. Do you think I should email him in a few days just to check on him? I'd hate to leave things the way they ended."

Megan thought for a moment.

"I don't know, Rache. Maybe you should just leave it be. But think on it a few days before you decide. Who knows, he might realize he overreacted and contact you to apologize. I'd give him some time."

"Sounds like a good idea." I took a deep breath. "What a day this has turned out to be," I said. "You want some hot chocolate and popcorn?"

"When have I ever turned down hot chocolate and popcorn?"

They were perfect on a cool autumn evening in New York. Megan and I enjoyed both as we watched some mindless television. Just before I got ready for bed, I received a text from Justin.

Justin: Good night, beautiful! I'll be dreaming of you.
Talk to you mañana.
Me: U'r welcome! Sweet dreams. :-)

Relaxing with Megan took my mind off of my conversation with Roger, but the text from Justin made my night. I nestled into my bed. I was hoping for some sweet dreams of my own.

CHAPTER 37

Justin

As I rode the elevator, I tapped my foot nervously. Until last week I had never really discussed my feelings with anyone. I certainly had never considered seeing a therapist. Especially to help me deal with my commitment issues so I could have a healthy relationship with a woman. I was counting the floors as the elevator ascended to the twentieth floor where Dr. Pamela Banks had her office.

Andrew said that she came highly recommended. Dr. Banks had a PhD in Psychology and specialized in relationships and couple's therapy. The elevator reached the twentieth floor and the doors opened. I took a deep breath and stepped out into the hallway. I checked the floor directory and headed left toward *Dr. Banks, PhD*'s office.

When I reached her suite, I opened the door to the reception/waiting area. There was a comfortable looking couch and chairs. The walls were painted a light mint color. Healing aloe or something like that. *Promoting a soothing environment,* I thought to myself.

"May I help you?" asked the receptionist.

"Yes. Justin Renaud. I have a ten o'clock appointment with Dr. Banks."

"Yes, Mr. Renaud. Here is some paperwork for you to fill out. Does your insurance have mental health coverage?"

"I'm not sure." I had no clue as it had never even occurred to me to ask.

"If you give me your card, I can run it and check for you. I'll also need a copy of a photo id."

I handed her my driver's license and insurance card. Then I sat in one of the comfy chairs and filled out the several forms on the clipboard. When I finished, I returned the paperwork to the receptionist.

"Thank you," she said taking the clipboard from me. "Good news. Your insurance does cover the visit. It will just be a fifty dollar copay."

She handed my insurance card and license back to me. I handed her my credit card. She swiped my card and had me sign the receipt.

"Thank you, Mr. Renaud. Please have a seat. Dr. Banks will be with you shortly."

"Thank you."

I sat back down and flipped through the stack of magazines on the table. *People, Esquire, TIME, Psychology Today, Sports Illustrated.* I settled on the *Sports Illustrated.* I was half way through an article when the door to Dr. Banks's office opened.

"Mr. Renaud."

I assumed that the woman who stood in the open doorway was Dr. Banks.

"Yes," I said as I put the magazine down and stood.

"I'm Dr. Banks. A pleasure to meet you." She extended her hand.

"Nice to meet you," I said as we shook hands.

"Please, come in," said Dr. Banks as she motioned for me to enter her office.

We went in and I looked around the office. Same soothing mint color on the walls. She had diplomas and awards hanging on the wall behind her desk. There was one of those psychologist couches on one side. There was also a sitting area with a couple of chairs.

Dr. Banks saw my eyes dart toward the couch and then back to the chairs.

"Where would you be most comfortable?" she asked me.

"I think the chairs," I replied.

"Very well. Please, have a seat."

We sat. She pulled out a notepad and rested it on her lap.

"I understand that you wish to speak with me about issues surrounding the relationship that your parents had and how that may be impacting your ability to establish a relationship."

"Yes."

"Very well. Can you tell me about your parents' marriage."

"They're divorced. They have been for several years now."

Dr. Banks scribbled some notes on her pad.

"Tell me about when they were married. What was that like for you?"

"It sucked. For me and my brothers. My parents fought constantly."

She scribbled more notes.

"Tell me more about that," she said.

"Not much more to tell. They fought all the time. Day and night. They grew to hate each other."

"Hate is a strong word. An even stronger emotion," said Dr. Banks.

"In my parents' case, I think it's appropriate. I don't ever remember them saying 'I love you' to each other . . ."

"What about to you? Your brothers?"

"Yes. My mom all the time. My dad not as much. A few times, maybe."

"Did you feel love from your father?"

"I'm not sure about the question."

"You said your mom told you she loved you all the time. Your dad a few times. Those are words. How did your mother and father make you feel?"

"I know my mom loves us, if that is what you are asking. She's very loving and caring."

"And your father?"

"I guess, in his own way he loves us. He doesn't talk about feelings. He didn't express how he felt very well."

"Did you feel love from him? No matter how he expressed it?"

"I suppose. Not like my mother. Not even close."

She scribbled some more notes on her pad.

"So, is that it? My dad didn't love me enough so I can't love women? I mean, like in a relationship?"

"It is too soon for us to know much of anything. But I would venture to guess that is part of it. Please, tell me more about your parents' marriage. You said they fought all the time. How did that make you feel?"

"I guess I'm a bit like my dad. Renaud men don't talk much about how they feel. Not in our DNA."

"Try. If we can't get to how you are feeling, then there will be little for us to explore."

I shifted uncomfortably in me seat. I crossed my legs. I tried to relax, but I felt stiff.

"When I was little, it scared me to hear them fight all the time. As I got older, it made me mad. Especially toward my dad. He could be a real jerk. I was happy when they got divorced because at least they wouldn't be fighting. They could get on with their lives."

"Tell me a little about your brothers."

I told her about Andrew, David, and Matthew. She asked if they had relationships. I wasn't sure what that had to do with me and my lack of relationships, but I went with it. She had the fancy degrees and was supposedly very good at what she did.

She scribbled more notes as I talked.

"What about you? Tell me about people you have dated," said Dr. Banks when I finished telling her about my brothers.

"I haven't."

"Pardon?" She raised an eyebrow like she didn't believe me.

She knew I had commitment issues, but I don't think she was expecting me to tell her that I never even dated.

"I haven't dated. I mean I've gone out with women. A lot of them, actually, but I've never dated any of them. Until very recently. The woman I'm trying to establish something with. She's the first woman I've 'dated,' if you will."

"Okay. We will get to your recent interest in a minute. So, even as a teenager or in college, you never went on a date?"

"Not exactly. I'd go out with someone one or two times. Maybe three. Never more than that."

She scribbled more notes.

"Do you try to avoid girls?"

"No. I don't avoid them at all. Like I said, I've been with lots of girls. Ever since I was a teenager. Casual always came easy. No dating, no commitments. Uncomplicated."

Dr. Banks wrote some more and nodded her head slightly as she did. A breakthrough?

She asked me more questions. It was getting very personal. I didn't mind sharing as much as I thought I would. I was offloading a lot of stuff all at once. When I finished, she asked me about Rachel.

"Can you tell me about the person you recently started seeing?"

"Rachel. She is amazing. She's nothing like any of the other women that I've been with. She captivated me from the very beginning. But I didn't plan on anything more with her than I had with anyone else."

"So what changed?"

"She refused my advances."

"And that had never happened before?"

"Occasionally I would get turned down. Not often, but it happened. But I always just moved on. There was always a 'yes' around the corner after a 'no.'"

"But not this time?"

"Rachel wanted no part of it. I knew she was attracted to me. There was a real chemistry between us. I figured I would wear her down."

"But Rachel was different? She said no, but you pursued her? You wanted to get a 'yes' out of her?"

"Yes. I did."

"And that was completely new for you?"

"Absolutely. Like I said, I had always about keeping things simple and uncomplicated. No commitment."

"Yes, we've established that. Tell me more about Rachel and your desire to be with her."

I continued telling Dr. Banks about the botched dinner date and all that happened after.

"Well, our time is up, but I think we have made very good progress for today," Dr. Banks announced at the end of the hour.

"So, what do you think?" I asked.

"I think we have identified some important issues. I'd like to continue our conversation. I sense a real willingness on your part."

"So how long before I am fixed?"

"It's not that you need 'fixing,' Mr. Renaud. You need help in dealing with your emotions and experiences in a healthy way so you can commit to and develop a healthy relationship. That takes some time. But this was a very good start. Does Rachel know you are here?"

"Yes. It was partly her idea. My brother Drew as well."

"Very good. Why don't you see how she feels about being a part of some of our conversations."

"I don't think she's the problem," I said.

"No. And neither are you. Again, you have some issues to work through. But you seem willing to do so. Much of the work you have to do on your own. But you are not alone in this. Rachel can, and should, be a part of the process."

"Okay. I'll ask her."

"Excellent. Why don't you set up another session on your way out. One more by yourself and then we can see about including Rachel."

I nodded. "Thank you," I said as I exited her office.

I made a follow-up appointment and then headed for the elevator. I was mentally spent. But also, strangely, feeling a bit liberated.

I had just spent an hour spilling intimate details and feelings with a total stranger. Granted, she was a highly regarded therapist. Still this was a big deal for me. Not only that, but I felt that it would actually be helpful. I was sensing that Rachel meant a lot more to me than I would have even thought possible a few days before.

CHAPTER 38

Rachel

I was looking forward to seeing Justin after work. He had his first session today with Dr. Banks. I was hoping it went well.

I arrived at *Renaud's* and approached Tank. He waved me through the VIP line. I thought he smiled at me. It was tough to tell with Tank.

I texted Justin I was at the restaurant. He asked me to meet him by the bar. When I got there, he was finishing a conversation with Nick, his head bartender, and Sam, his assistant manager.

"Okay. I'll check in later," Justin said to Nick and Sam. He then turned toward me and gave me a light kiss on the lips.

"Hey, beautiful," he said.

"Hey, to you," I said.

Two women approached Justin from the other side. Two blonds. They looked like twins. Blond One and Blond Two. They were busty, curvy, and up to no good. *Better look someplace else*, I thought.

"Hi, Justin," said blond one.

"Hi, handsome," said blond two.

"Good evening, ladies. Enjoying yourselves?"

"Very much," said blond one.

"Good. Have a nice evening," Justin said as he took me by the hand and started to walk away."

"Wait," said blond two. "Can we get your number?"

Justin spun around. "Ladies, I would like you to meet my girlfriend, Rachel."

They both looked me up and down. They would have completely dismissed me if it were not for the fact Justin introduced me as his girlfriend. *Girlfriend.* That was the first time Justin ever uttered the word. And he said it about me.

"She's very pretty," said blond one.

"Yes, she is. And we are on our way to dinner," replied Justin. "My apologies, ladies, but I'm not available. Not tonight. Not any night. I'm with Rachel."

"You sure?" asked blond one. It was like they were a tag team.

"Positive. Good night."

Justin and I turned and headed toward the front door.

"Girlfriend?" I asked.

"Well, yes. You do want to be my girlfriend, don't you?"

"I'm just surprised to hear you say it."

"Me too. But I'm having breakthroughs all over the place this week," he said as we stepped out into the evening air. "I'll tell you all about it over dinner."

We had a wonderful dinner at Bouley's to make up for our failed first date. Justin then asked me back to his place.

He had a nice one bedroom apartment. It was in an old brownstone, furnished with nice brown leather dark wood furniture to match.

There were several pictures of him with three guys I assumed were his brothers. They sure looked like brothers. I saw some photographs of him with the same three guys and a woman whom I assumed was his mom. I didn't see any of someone who could be his dad.

Justin saw me looking at the pictures. He picked up one of the frames off the table.

"These are my brothers and my mom. That's Andrew, next to him is David, and there's Matthew."

"I gathered they were your brothers. You all look very similar."

"Yep. The Renaud boys have the same good looks," he said with a grin.

"I assume they share your modesty as well," I teased.

"No. That is just me," he teased back.

Then he kissed me gently on the lips. Oh, how I had fallen in love with his delectable pink lips. So full and soft, yet still masculine.

After some light kissing Justin made us dessert out of fresh strawberries and chocolate ice cream. "The strawberries are from upstate. Last of the season. And the ice cream from a dairy farm near the strawberry patch."

"Strawberry picking and dairy ice cream? I didn't take you for an upstate type of guy."

"Compliments of David. He spoke at some conference and picked them up on his way home."

"I think David is a good influence for you."

I was feeling even better about being with Justin. He told me over dinner about his session with Dr. Banks and he seemed open about the entire process. He told me how she asked me to join at some point. I immediately agreed. Anything to help.

I was really falling for Justin. I was discovering a tenderness and a sense of humor in him. And, amazingly, based on our first few meetings, his desire to move toward commitment with me. I wanted a relationship with him to succeed. He definitely started as Mr. Wrong, but that was falling away and he was emerging as a solid candidate for Mr. Right.

We kissed again and my heart was fluttering. I was comfortable where I was. Justin and I felt right together.

CHAPTER 39

The following weeks passed quickly. I was busy rolling out the restaurant *Renaud's* campaign. By every measure, it was a success from day one. The lines outside grew longer and the buzz surrounding the restaurant truly made it the hottest new night restaurant in Manhattan.

Justin continued his sessions with Dr. Banks. I joined for a couple's session. It seemed only fitting. We were becoming a true couple.

Justin was coming to terms with his parents terrible relationship and what that did to him. He was gaining valuable perspective and learning that he could have a very different, positive, and healthy relationship. We both benefited. In more ways than one.

We reached an important milestone in placing toothbrushes at each others apartments. Megan was even warming toward Justin. I had reached out to Roger, but he never responded. I had heard through mutual friends that he had been back in New York a few days.

I would have liked to think that he and I could one day be friends. But I guessed only time would tell if he would ever be comfortable with that. I figured I simply had to give him time. If he wanted to be friends, he knew how to get in touch with me.

I was getting ready to go out with Justin. He was taking me to a Knicks game. I'd never really followed basketball, but I was looking forward to sharing this experience with Justin. Megan had just left for dinner with Zack. I pulled on the Knicks shirt Justin had bought for me.

I heard the doorbell ring. Justin was early. I smiled as I walked toward the door. I had just seen him the night before, but I couldn't wait to see him again. We were in that phase of our relationship.

I opened the door. It was Roger.

"Roger, what are you doing here?"

"I felt bad about the way I hung up on you and ignored your email. Can I come in for a minute?"

"I'm leaving in a few minutes for the Knicks game. But, sure, come on in for a minute."

I let him into the apartment and closed the door behind him.

"I can't stop thinking about you. About what we said on the phone."

"Roger, I hope that we can be friends, but that is all we can ever be."

"I just can't accept that, Rachel."

I didn't like Roger's tone of voice. It was very direct. Very matter of fact.

"Well, you are going to have to. I'm sorry, I don't mean to be rude, but I need to finish getting ready for the game."

"You look ready to me. Nice fitting jeans. Cute little Knicks t-shirt. It shows your perky breasts. Remember how I used to caress your breasts?"

"Roger, you are making me uncomfortable. I need to ask you to leave."

I reached for the door. Roger shoved my arm away.

"No one is going anywhere." Roger locked the door and the security chain.

"What are you doing? You need to leave."

"I already told you. No one is going anywhere."

Roger's tone was chilling. Like it had been on the phone a few weeks earlier. When I was glad that he wasn't in the same room with me. But now he was standing right in front of me. In a locked apartment.

"Roger, please. You need to think this through."

"Oh, I already have. I know exactly what I am going to do. And you are going to love it. Just like old times."

Roger moved closer towards me. He was well into my personal space.

"Roger, no."

"Yes." Roger grabbed my arm hard and pulled me into him.

I opened my mouth to scream, but Roger forced his hand over my mouth. He spun me around. He made sure to keep a firm grip on my arm with one hand and my mouth covered with his other.

Tears welled up in my eyes. My body trembled. Roger was moving us toward the hallway that led to my bedroom. I tried to break free, but Roger was too strong.

I heard a key in the door. The lock turned and the door opened and then caught on the security chain.

"Rachel, why is the door chained?" It was Megan. Roger and I were already out of sight of the door. My heart was pounding. I struggled harder to break free. I tried to twist my head out of his grip so I could yell.

Roger just held on tighter. "Stop struggling or it will be a lot worse for you. And for Megan."

CHAPTER 40

When Roger showed up at my apartment I never expected he would try to harm me. The tone of his voice on the phone a few weeks ago concerned me, but I never thought he would ever try to harm me. To be honest, I didn't think much about it when he showed up at my door.

He had greeted me like the Roger I had known. He wanted to apologize for getting upset. I quickly realized that was just so he could get in my apartment. I was terrified about what he might to do me. And, to Megan.

She was now trying to remove the security chain from the door.

Roger had covered my mouth with his hand so I couldn't scream. His other hand was like a vice grip on my arm. I tried to break free, but Roger was too strong for me. He was forcing me down the hallway toward my bedroom.

"Rachel, are you okay," called Megan from the hallway. I could hear her struggling to remove the security chain to open the door all the way. "Why is the door chained?! Rachel!"

I struggled harder to break free, but Roger tightened his grip. Tears were freely flowing from my eyes.

"I told you to stop struggling," said Roger as he shoved me toward my bedroom.

"I've called the police," yelled Megan from the hallway. "They will be here any minute."

"Megan, what is going on?" I heard Justin's voice from the hallway.

"The door's chained. Something's wrong," Megan answered.

I heard a forceful kick against the door and the security chain tear from the wall. The door crashed open. Roger quickly turned his head toward the noise and then he shoved me into my bedroom. He started to push the door shut with the heel of his right foot when it swung in and knocked us both to the floor.

I looked up and Justin came rushing into the room and pinned Roger to the floor. He grabbed both his arms so he could not move.

"Are you okay?" asked Justin.

"I think so," I answered through my tears.

"Did he hurt you in any way?" Justin asked as he pressed down hard on Roger.

"Not really. He didn't get the chance to do anything other than grab me and cover my mouth," I replied as I sat up.

"He put his hands on you. That's too much," replied Justin.

Justin pressed his knee hard into Roger's back. Roger let out a groan. Other than that, Roger made no noise and did not move. Justin had him securely pinned to the floor.

Megan rushed into my room.

"The police are on their way," she said. She helped me up off the floor.

"What happened? Are you okay?" Megan looked down at Roger pinned to the floor underneath Justin.

"Is that Roger?"

I nodded. Megan helped me over to the bed. We both sat.

"Do you have handcuffs?" asked Justin.

Megan gave Justin a look. I was still too stunned to react.

"What kind of stuff do you think Rachel is into?" Megan asked Justin.

"Just would be helpful so I don't have to hold this scumbag much longer."

"No. Sorry. No handcuffs," I finally said.

"Hello," we heard someone call from the living room. "Someone call the police?"

Megan got off my bed and went into the hallway.

"In here," she called out.

A moment later, two police officers stepped into the doorway of my bedroom. Our doorman, Frank stood behind them. They looked down at Justin who had Roger pinned to the floor.

"This guy attacked my girlfriend," said Justin.

"We got here just in time," added Megan.

One of the police officers walked over and helped Justin lift Roger off the floor. He had Roger lean against the wall and patted him down. He placed Roger in handcuffs and read him the Miranda Rights. Then he led him out of my bedroom.

"Which one of you was the alleged victim?" asked the other police officer.

"Nothing 'alleged' about it! That scumbag went after her!" protested Justin.

"Just a moment, sir," said the officer.

"I am, officer," I said.

"Did the man attack you?" the officer asked.

"He grabbed me and covered my mouth," I said.

"Did he hurt you in any way?" asked the officer.

"He grabbed my arm pretty tight. Other than that, no. But he threatened me."

"In what way?" the officer asked.

"He indicated something bad would happen to me. And to Megan." I started sobbing.

"Do we have to do this now?" Megan asked as she put her arm around my shoulder.

"We will need to get a full statement for our report," replied the officer. "But we can go sit in the other room if that makes it easier."

I nodded my head. We went and sat at the kitchen table.

CHAPTER 41

The police officer took my statement and confirmed that I wanted to press charges. He also got statements from Justin and Megan. He gave me his card in case I thought of anything else and then told me that someone would be in touch.

Frank apologized for letting Roger into the building. He told us that he remembered Roger, that Roger had told him that he just moved back to New York, and that Roger told him that he was getting together with me and a bunch of other friends for the evening. Frank said there was nothing suspicious about what he said or the way that he acted. I could tell that Frank felt terrible.

I told him not to worry. Roger had me fooled as well. I mean, I actually let him into the apartment. The police officer suggested that the building implement a more stringent security policy. Frank agreed that from that point forward, he and the other doormen would check with residents before letting anyone into the building.

Megan let Frank and the police officer out and then locked the door behind them. The security chain was ripped from the wall, but our deadbolt was still in good shape. When Megan returned to the kitchen, she said she would call maintenance to get the security chain replaced.

Justin sat next to me at the kitchen table and placed his hand on top of mine.

"I don't know what would have happened if you and Megan hadn't shown up," I said.

"I don't even want to think about that," said Megan.

Megan's cellphone rang. She glanced at the screen.

"Oh, I forgot to call Zack," she said as she picked up the phone and walked into the living room.

Megan had been on her way to meet Zack for a date.

"We are lucky that Megan forgot her phone and came back for it," said Justin.

"That and you showing up," I said.

"Megan was able to unlock the door with her key. Without that, I wouldn't have been able to get into your apartment as quickly as I did. Sorry about the chain, by the way."

I smiled at him. It was the first time that I felt relaxed since the whole ordeal with Roger had started.

"I'm sorry that we missed the start of the Knicks game. We can still go if you want," I said.

"No. There will be other games. I think it's better if we just stay in tonight. How about I order us a pizza and we see what's on TV? Maybe a good comedy," he suggested.

"That sounds perfect," I said.

"Do you think Megan will join us?" he asked.

"I don't know. I think she should still go on her date with Zack. I'm fine with you here with me," I said.

Almost on cue, Megan walked into the kitchen.

"Zack said that he hopes you are doing okay," she said.

"Are you still going to see him tonight?" I asked. "I think you should. Justin is staying, I'll be okay."

"I feel like I should stay. I mean, I feel strange leaving you to go on a date after what happened," she replied.

"No. I insist. Fortunately, you guys showed up when you did. I was really rattled by the whole thing, but I am feeling better now. You going out with Zack will help get everything back to normal that much faster."

"You sure? Zack completely understands. So do I."

"No. You should go. Really, I will be fine. Justin and I are getting a pizza and are going to watch a movie on Netflix."

"You're positive?"

"Yes. Positive. I swear. Please go and have a fun night with Zack."

Megan could tell that I was serious and that I was feeling better. She relented and agreed to go on her date with Zack.

"Say, Rache?" she said as she picked up her purse from the table.

"Yeah?"

"Sorry about Roger," she said.

"It's not your fault."

"No, I mean about trying to convince you to consider getting back with him. I was, obviously, wrong about that. Wrong about him."

"Megs, I don't want you to blame yourself about any of this. There was no way to know he was going to act the way he did. I certainly didn't see it coming. How could you?"

"I wouldn't be able to live with myself if he had done anything to you. It's bad enough that he terrorized you they way he did. I can't even imagine . . ."

"It's okay, Megs. I'm fine. Let's not dwell on this. Okay?"

Megan paused for a moment. I could tell she still felt some guilt. She had nothing to feel guilty about. She was my best friend and always wanted what was best for me. There was no way for either of us to suspect Roger would turn on me the way that he did.

"Okay?" I asked again. I hugged her.

"Okay," she finally said as she hugged me back.

"Thanks for coming back for your phone," I said.

"At first I was mad at myself for forgetting it. I was halfway to the subway when I realized that I didn't have it. I was upset about having to come back for it. I almost didn't. But then I heard your voice reminding me we should never be without our phones. You know, in case of an emergency. So I came back for it."

"Well, I'm sure glad you did."

"And I'm glad Justin showed up when he did. . ."

"That too," I said. "Now go, have a good time with Zack. Just be sure to call when you get there."

"Actually, I'm going to have Zack pick me up here," she said.

"Even better," I said.

"You two want to join us for pizza before you go out?" asked Justin.

I had almost forgotten he was sitting at the kitchen table.

"No, thanks. You kids enjoy. I'm going to wait for Zack in the lobby. Frank probably still feels really bad about letting Roger up. I'll let him know everything is okay."

"I'll order the pizza," said Justin. "Any requests?"

"I'd like green peppers on my half," I said.

"You can eat half a pizza?" Justin teased.

"Tonight. Yes."

"Green peppers it is," he said.

Megan left and Justin ordered our pizza. It wasn't the night I had planned, but I knew how fortunate I was. I also realized how safe I felt with Justin. I was glad he was with me.

CHAPTER 42

Justin and I finished our pizza and settled on the couch to find a movie to watch. We found *When Harry Met Sally* on Netflix.

"Ooh, I love that movie," I said. "Do you mind if we watch it?"

"No. Whatever you want to watch is okay with me."

"Wow, very agreeable. First we miss the Knicks game and now you have to watch a chick flick. I'm impressed, Mr. Renaud."

"You've had a tough night." He kissed me on the forehead.

"I did. But it is better now. I'm glad you are here."

"Me, too."

"It's interesting how people can change," I said. "When I was with . . . I can't even say his name now. Anyway, when I was with him, he seemed so nice. He was a good boyfriend. He did seem a bit strange on the phone a few weeks ago, but I never imagined he was capable of what happened tonight."

"There was probably something there already. Maybe he hid it well. Maybe as long as things went the way he wanted, he could hide it."

"But he didn't go all crazy when we broke up," I said.

"Didn't you say he made that decision?"

"More or less. He had already decided to take the job. He wanted me to move. I didn't. So we broke up. Why didn't he turn on me then?"

"I don't know. There must be more to it. All I know is he tried to hurt you tonight. He needs to spend time in jail. We'll work hard to make sure he does. The only reason I didn't beat the crap out of him was to not complicate the police investigation. I didn't want to give him any chance of coming at me with anything."

"This is one time I am glad you decided not to complicate your life," I said.

"I've come to appreciate you complicating my life," Justin replied.

"See, people changing. I'm glad with how you are changing. But, like you said, it was probably always there," I commented.

"You mean my wanting commitment? Wanting a relationship?"

"Sort of. I think at least you were not as opposed to the idea of commitment and a relationship as you thought you were. What was it Dr. Banks said? . . . You were using a lack of commitment as a defense against the type of bad relationship your parents had. What you witnessed in their relationship at a young age colored your perceptions. You had no reference point for what a healthy relationship looked like."

"Until I met you," Justin said.

"Pretty amazing turnaround, I would say."

"I'm a work in progress. If I'm honest, it still scares me. I don't want to be like my dad. I don't want to treat you the way he treated my mom."

"You have a recognition your dad probably didn't. It makes you different from him. It is why you can do this."

"I'm certainly trying," Justin said.

"Yes, you are. And I'm grateful. Just think, we'd be missing out on snuggling on the couch and watching *When Harry Met Sally* together," I teased.

"Just think."

I gave Justin a soft kiss on the lips. I didn't think I could ever grow tired of his wonderful lips.

"I'm glad you are here," I whispered into his ear.

"I'm not going anywhere," he replied.

CHAPTER 43

"So this is Rachel. It is so wonderful to meet you," said Andrew Renaud.

Andrew agreed to meet to give me an idea of the city's charges against Roger. We were meeting for lunch at a cafe near Andrew's office.

"It is nice to meet you. Thank you for agreeing to offer your insight," I said as we sat down at our table.

"You are most welcome. Truth be told, I've been hounding Justin to meet you. I only wish it were under different circumstances."

He was dressed in an expensive suite and was impeccably groomed. But there was nothing stuffy about him. He was relaxed and easy-going.

"We understand that you are not a prosecutor and that you don't even handle criminal law, but . . ." began Justin.

"I am an attorney and my advice is free," finished Andrew.

"I was going to put it slightly nicer than that. But I suppose that pretty much sums it up," replied Justin.

"I just appreciate having any legal insight in what to expect," I said.

"Well, based on what Justin told me, I'm afraid I can't offer much hope for the eventual outcome. Now, don't get me wrong, I believe he will be found guilty and convicted. But I foresee a problem with the charges and likely conviction," said Andrew.

"So, wait a minute. Are you saying that scumbag doesn't get put away for a long time?" Justin's neck veins throbbed.

"The reality is he will be charged with assault in the third degree. Like I said, he should be convicted. But it is only a misdemeanor, not a felony. In New York that carries a maximum of one year in jail," stated Andrew.

"Just a year?! For terrorizing Rachel the way he did?!" Justin was beside himself.

"Justin, I know it is upsetting, but I'm telling you what is likely to happen from a legal perspective."

"It doesn't seem right," Justin continued.

"Unfortunately, those are the limits of the charges and possible conviction. What is worse is if it is a first offense he probably won't get any jail time. Most likely a three-year probation," said Andrew.

"That is unbelievable," said Justin.

"Justin, I'm as upset about this as you are," I said. "In fact, think about how it makes me feel. But we asked Andrew for his legal opinion. I wanted to know what the possible outcome is. Even what is most probable."

"I know. I'm sorry. I just want him to be punished for this. And I want Rachel to be safe from him."

"I did receive an email and voice mail from Roger's ex-girlfriend in Dallas," I said. "She had sent it to my work contacts, the only information she could find for me. She warned me Roger had seemed obsessed with getting back together with me. She said he seemed crazed with the idea. It frightened her a little. Unfortunately, I didn't get them until after the fact."

I had told Justin about the email and voice mail messages. It was part of his being so wound up over the situation. He felt helpless.

"Those can certainly be entered into evidence and considered," added Andres. "It still isn't likely to change the end result. Probably help with a conviction, but not likely to change sentencing. Roger may also accept a plea to the charge. He might get probation," said Andrew.

"This really stinks," said Justin.

"It does," agreed Andrew. "I wish I could offer better news. Justice is supposed to be blind. To go with what is presented. Sometimes people get charged on bogus charges because accusations get trumped-up, or the accusers are connected, or it's political, or all of the above. Sometimes people should get a greater punishment but the law limits what can be done. The system isn't perfect. But what is?"

I could tell that Andrew hated to be the bearer of such bad news. But he obviously understood the frustration with the situation and what was possible within the legal system.

We finished lunch on a lighter note as we chatted a bit about Justin, Andrew, and their brothers David and Matthew. I also shared a little about my siblings. I liked Andrew. It was obvious that Justin looked up to him and that the two were very close. Andrew invited us to dinner for later in the week and he also made me agree to attending a Knicks game with all four Renaud brothers. I told him I already had the shirt so I needed to put it to good use.

When all was said and done, Roger accepted a plea to the charge of assault in the third degree. He received two years probation and a fine of $1,000. His attorney arranged for him to serve his probation in Dallas.

Apparently, Roger's employer seemed eager for him to return to his job in Dallas rather than transfer back to New

York. I was sure they didn't want any negative PR hovering over their office. I had a feeling Roger wasn't likely to be asked to return to New York any time soon.

I would have liked to have seen a little more of a punishment, but I understood what the law was. At least there was acknowledgment Roger had done something wrong. Even a slap on the wrist was better than nothing. More importantly, Roger was no longer in New York. The distance in miles would help me in moving on.

It also removed the possibility of Justin kicking Roger's butt. He was still upset Roger never saw the inside of a jail cell. But with Roger most of the way across the country, Justin was dealing with it a little better.

CHAPTER 44

Justin

In many ways, I was miles from where I had been before Rachel and I got together. Rachel was the most amazing woman I had ever met. I trusted what we were together. I trusted what we could have.

Am I falling in love with Rachel? I asked myself. I wasn't certain because I had never felt like this before. Sure, I loved my mother and my brothers. In a way, I even loved my dad. But I had never been in love with someone.

I had been right all along. Rachel Cooper was trouble for me. She had complicated my life. But now I welcomed it. I liked it. I might even love it.

CHAPTER 45

Freshly showered and dressed, I walked down the hall to my office. I turned on my computer and waited for it to boot up. I glanced at the picture of me with my brothers and mom on my desk. I decided I needed a picture of Rachel. I really was in deep.

"No turning back, Renaud," I said to myself.

My computer came to life and I started to log on. There was a knock on my office door.

"Come in," I said.

The door opened and Nick, my head bartender, was standing there.

"Can I speak to you for a minute?" he asked.

"Of course, come on in."

Nick stepped into my office and sat in the chair opposite my desk. He seemed hesitant. Almost nervous.

"What's up, man? You seem a bit out of sorts," I said.

"Look, Justin, there is no easy way to say this," Nick said.

"Just say it."

"I'm turning in my resignation, effective immediately," said Nick.

My mouth fell open. I couldn't believe it. Nick was the first guy I had hired to work at *Renaud's*. He was an excellent bartender.

"Nick, why?"

"It's not that I don't appreciate working here. I do. I just feel like it is time for me to move on. I want to open my own bar. You know, be the boss. Reap the rewards of the profits."

"Okay, I get that. But I hate to lose you from the restaurant. Do you have a plan in place? This seems awfully sudden."

"No. not yet. I just decided to go for it not that long ago. I do have some cash saved up and some people interested in investing."

"You don't need to quit just yet. Let me hear your plan. Maybe I can help you out with opening the bar. My brothers and I may even want to invest."

"I appreciate that, Justin. Really, I do. But I want to do this all on my own. It needs to be my thing. If you help or invest, it will be more an extension of you and the restaurant rather than of me and my vision."

"It doesn't have to be like that."

"I still prefer to do this on my own. I've never accomplished much so this is important to me. That I do it on my own."

"None of us truly do anything on our own. We all get help, from somebody or somewhere, along the way. Doesn't diminish the accomplishment any."

"Look, Justin, I really just need to do this my way. I hope you understand."

"Okay. If that is how you want to play it. I respect your decision."

"Thanks for understanding."

"So, what about tonight? It's hard to imagine how the bar is going to run without you behind it."

"It's a great bar tending crew. They will be fine."

"Just don't try to steal them away."

"Can't make any promises. It's business. You know?"

"I guess. Just give me enough time to replace them."

I didn't like Nick leaving. I especially didn't like him leaving so abruptly. Just walking out the door like that wasn't cool. It didn't set well with me. But I saw no need to bust Nick's chops over it. Getting upset wouldn't change his mind.

I shook Nick's hand and wished him luck. I told him to keep in touch and let me know if he changed his mind and if there was anything that I could do to help. He nodded and then left.

I knew that I had great bartenders besides Nick. That wasn't the point. The point was *Renaud's* was very busy and we needed each and every one of the bartenders pretty much every night.

I would have to start looking for another bartender to hire. My more immediate problem was what to do about the fact the restaurant would be opening in four hours. *Sam*, I thought. Sam, my assistant manager, had been a bartender before I hired him to help me manage the restaurant. I'd have Sam fill in behind the bar until we could hire Nick's replacement.

With that problem solved, for the moment at least, I turned my attention to my afternoon work load. I was behind on reconciling the restaurant's bank account. I decided to add hiring a bookkeeper to the list of things I needed to do.

I logged into our bank account and began reviewing our statements. Something didn't seem right. I pulled up our internal financial records. Things weren't adding up. Literally.

I called David.

"What's up, Justin?" said David when he answered the phone.

"When was the last time you reviewed the restaurant's financial records?" I asked him.

"Month or so, I guess. Why?"

"The bank account deposits are less than our internal records indicate," I said as I compared both files.

"Did you check with the bank? There may have been an error when a deposit was made."

"It would have to have been an error over several deposits. The difference is too great to be just one deposit," I replied.

"Do you have the actual deposit slips?" David asked.

"Hold on a second," I said as I opened my desk drawer and pulled out the folder where we put our deposit slips.

I flipped through the deposit slips for the past month.

"The deposit slips and the bank statements match. They are showing the same deposit amounts on the same dates."

"That's problematic," said David. "The registers in the restaurant are all computers tied into the central accounting software. They record transactions real-time. Even for cash payments."

"So what are you saying, David? Is someone skimming cash before it gets deposited in the bank?"

"Unfortunately, it seems the most likely scenario. A lot of people pay with credit and debit cards today, even for small purchases. But enough people still pay with cash, especially for before dinner drinks at the bar. Skimming a little here and a little there would add up over time," said David.

"Yeah, especially as much business as we have been doing," I said.

"Any idea who it might be?" asked David.

"I think it was Nick," I said. I didn't want to believe it, but it made the most sense. "He just quit. Said he was going to open his own bar. Told me he had some cash saved up."

"Sure sounds like he would be a prime suspect," said David. "Now we just need to prove it. Which might be tough to do."

"Unless we can catch him in the act," I said. "We've got security cameras all over the restaurant. They are always running. They are digital and memory is cheap, so I just leave them running."

"Wouldn't Nick have known how to avoid the cameras?" asked David.

"Maybe not. He knew we had them and where they are located. But I don't think he knew they run 24/7. Probably assumed they went off after the restaurant closed."

"Well, we can only hope that is the case and we have a video record of him, or whoever it is, pocketing the cash," said David.

"I'll check the recordings and let you know what I find," I said.

"Okay. Talk to you later," said David.

We hung up. I opened the surveillance footage file on my computer. I started with the days just before the deposits in question. I forwarded to times after closing. I figured that was the most likely time where Nick, or whoever, would pocket the cash.

It didn't take me long to find some solid evidence. The video showed Nick clearly stashing wads of cash into his backpack. All of it had happened after closing. Nick was cautious and discreet, but the video didn't lie.

Nick either figured that the surveillance cameras were not running between closing and when we all left or he just hadn't been thinking about it. I always thought Nick was smarter than that. I also thought he was honest and could be trusted. Either way, he had stolen from the restaurant.

I was picking up the phone to call David and then the police. I hung up the phone. As the video continued to run, I saw two men enter into the picture. I didn't recognize either one of them. They spoke to Nick and then Nick handed them the backpack. As soon as they had the backpack, they left.

A payoff of some sorts? Was Nick working for someone else to steal from me? All that was clear was that Nick was stealing money and handing it over to two guys. I called David back and told him what I had seen on the video. He agreed that I should call the police and provide the video as evidence. Hopefully we would discover who the other two guys were and get to the bottom of what was going on.

I hung up with David and looked up the number for the local police precinct. As I was dialing, the front door buzzer on my phone rang. I checked the front door video and saw a man in a suit standing outside the door. I hit the intercom button.

"Hello," I said.

"Yes, I am Detective Rivers with NYPD. I am here to see Mr. Justin Renaud." He held his badge up to the camera so I could see it. "I have a few questions about a Nicholas Peters."

"I am Justin Renaud. Yes, Nick is, or was, my head bartender. Let me buzz you in and I will meet you downstairs."

"Thank you," said Detective Rivers.

I buzzed the door open and then headed downstairs to meet Detective Rivers. It sure seemed that there was more to Nick stealing cash from the restaurant and handing it over to the two men in the surveillance video. The police already seemed to have an investigation underway.

CHAPTER 46

"Mr. Renaud, we have reason to believe Mr. Nicholas Peters is involved in a money laundering operation out of your restaurant," said Detective Rivers as we sat in my booth.

"Have you noticed anything out of the ordinary with restaurant financial accounts?"

"Yes. As a matter of fact, I just noticed irregularities this morning. I also have video surveillance footage of Nick stealing cash and then handing it to two men in a backpack."

"We will need copies of the financial records in question as well as the surveillance video," replied Detective Rivers.

"No problem. I'll get you copies."

"Do you have any idea who the other two men in the video are?" asked Detective Rivers.

"Not a clue. And how would Nick get caught up in money laundering?"

"That's what we would like to know. We suspect the two men work for a local crime boss. Pretty small time operation, but he launders a little through several different reputable establishments. A little here and a little there adds up."

"I thought laundering happened through front business owned by or connected to the criminals," I said. "Why my restaurant and other local businesses?"

"That is the part we are not sure about. There is some connection between the crime ring and the other establishments. We haven't established any connection to your restaurant. Other than Nick."

I shook my head in disbelief.

"But this is an ongoing investigation," continued Detective Rivers.

"Wait a second, you don't suspect me or someone other than Nick as being involved in this? Do you?" I asked.

"We don't know much beyond what we have shared with you. And, no, you are not a suspect. But it is an ongoing investigation and we can't rule out others being involved. Your cooperation with our investigation will help us, hopefully, wrap up our investigation sooner and get those involved."

"Whatever I can do to help. I, obviously, don't like the idea my restaurant is involved in any sort of criminal activity."

"How soon can you get us copies of your financial records and the surveillance video?"

"I can save most everything to a flash drive and make copies of the deposit slips for you right now."

I gave copies of all the files, video, and deposit slips to Detective Rivers. He gave me his card and told me call him if I discovered anything else. He told me he would be in touch when he knew more. Until then, he told me not to say anything to the staff about the investigation.

After Detective Rivers left, I went behind the bar and poured myself a drink. I had an hour before the staff would arrive to get the restaurant ready to open for the night. I downed my drink and headed back upstairs.

I walked past my office and down the hall to the suite. I went in and flopped down on the couch. I felt a headache coming on. I decided to shut my eyes for a few minutes to settle my mind.

CHAPTER 47

Rachel

"No way," said Megan.

"I know, it is hard to believe," I said. I had just finished telling Megan about Nick and the police investigation.

"The police have Nick in custody, but he isn't talking. His lawyer said Nick was being used."

"What does Justin think?" asked Megan.

"He doesn't know what to think. He feels betrayed by Nick. But he is at a loss as to who Nick's involved with or why."

"It has been crazy the past month or so," remarked Megan. "First the whole ordeal with your crazy ex and now this with Renaud's."

"I know. And I'm worried what it is all doing to Justin," I said.

"How so? I get he is upset about what is going on at the restaurant, but everything is still okay between you two. Right?"

"That's what I'm not sure about. Our business meetings are little more than that lately. We, of course, are still getting together outside of work, but it isn't the same. He seems a little distant."

"Have you talked to him about it?"

"Yes. He said he is just distracted by what is going on at the restaurant and why Nick would steal from him."

"Sounds plausible to me. You're not so sure?" asked Megan.

"It's just he has come so far in trusting a relationship. In letting me into his life. It feels like he's backing away. Maybe our relationship isn't going as well as I thought it was."

"Try not reading too much into it, Rache. It's not like he's suggesting you two take a break or anything like that."

"No. I just wish that he would let me be more a part of what he is going through."

"It's hard for him. He is getting used to what being in a relationship is like. I think you need to give him a little more slack than most guys," said Megan.

"Amazing," I said with a smile.

"What? I know I was wrong about Roger but . . ."

"No. It's not that. It is just amazing what a one-eighty you have made concerning Justin."

"Well, I think he has earned it," Megan replied.

"You're right. He has. And you are also correct in that I need to give him more slack on this. I just want us to continue building a strong relationship. I really like him."

"Do you think you are getting ready to use the 'L' word?" asked Megan.

"I think I am feeling it. I don't want to freak him out though. With someone else it probably wouldn't be too soon, but with Justin . . ."

"I get it. But, Rache, this is huge. Just knowing you feel it."

"I know. I only hope he might start feeling the same way."

"He'd be crazy not to," said Megan.

"Perhaps. But what I know for sure is Roger was enough of crazy for me."

"For us all. Just keep taking it a day at a time with Justin. You'll know when the time is right. So will he. You just may need to wait a little longer with him."

"Speaking of Justin, I need to run. I'm meeting him at the restaurant and we are going to dinner. I'm taking him out to try to take his mind off of things."

"Have fun."

CHAPTER 48

Justin

"Detective Rivers, Drew, Dave," I said as Detective Rivers and two of my brothers walked into Renaud's.

"Can we talk in private?" asked Detective Rivers.

"Sure. Let's go to my office."

Once we were in my office, Detective Rivers closed my door. He stood against the wall. It always made me uneasy when someone stood against the wall to have a conversation with me. I'm not sure why. I was particularly troubled by Detective Rivers. His body language suggested that it was bad news.

Drew and Dave sat. They hadn't said a word. They looked troubled. And where was Matt?

I sat behind my desk. I figured it was best that I was in a chair for whatever was coming.

"We've had a break in the case," he said.

"And?"

"You're not going to like it."

"What is going on?" I asked as I looked back and forth between Detective Rivers and my brothers.

"Justin, you need to keep calm about this," said Drew.

"Will somebody please just tell me what is going on?"

Detective Rivers looked over at Drew and Dave. They looked back at Detective Rivers. He nodded his head toward Drew.

"Justin," said Drew, "Detective Rivers believes that Matt is involved in stealing the money from the restaurant."

"What?! That is insane!" I said.

"We thought so too," said Dave. "But there is pretty compelling evidence that he is connected to the two guys who Nick had been giving money to."

"What kind of evidence?" I asked.

"Phone calls. Text messages. Deposits of cash into Matt's bank account that closely resembles the amount stolen from the restaurant. Minus payment to the two goons," said Detective Rivers.

"I don't believe it. Someone is setting Matt up. Maybe it's Nick. Maybe someone else, but Matt wouldn't do that. He's our brother," I protested.

"We didn't want to believe it either, Justin. But . . . Matt confessed to us," said Drew.

"He what? Drew what do you mean?"

"Apparently, the hotel is being sold. The new owners have announced they are bringing in new management. Matt was out of a job. He said there weren't any good jobs open in the city in hotel management. It's very competitive . . ."

"So? All of a sudden that makes Matt a crook?" I asked.

"It's not that simple," said Dave.

The room fell silent. Detective Rivers, Drew, and Dave all knew more. They hesitated to tell me. I wasn't sure that I wanted to know.

"Matt had been laundering money through the hotel for several months," said Detective Rivers. "Nick had been a bartender at the hotel . . ."

"I know that. Matt recommended Nick for the job here," I said.

"Yes. We know. Matt wanted Nick here. Nick was part of the money laundering at the hotel. Matt knew the hotel was being sold and he would likely be out of a job . . ."

"So he decided to set up shop here?" I said.

"In a manner of speaking, yes," said Detective Rivers.

"Matt is the guy you had been watching?" I asked.

"Yes. We've been investigating him for a number of months. We'd been watching Nick since we suspected a connection. Then Nick started working here. So we watched a little longer."

"When did you guys find out?" I asked Drew and Dave.

"Just a little while ago when Detective Rivers contacted us and went over the evidence. We had a chance to speak with Matt. Justin, we're sorry, he admitted to everything. One of the defense attorney's at my firm will represent him. We'll try to get him the lightest sentence we can. Hope for release on good behavior and get him some help," said Drew.

To be honest, I hadn't even thought that far. I thought Nick betraying me was bad enough. Now I had learned that one of my own brothers was behind the whole thing.

"Why didn't Matt just come to us for help?" I asked.

"We don't know," said Drew.

"We asked him that very question," said Dave. "He didn't have an answer for us."

"This has been a hell of a month," I said. "If you don't need anything from me, I need some time alone."

"No. We don't anything more from you right now," said Detective Rivers.

"Justin, you shouldn't be alone right now. Let's go somewhere and talk," said Drew.

"No. I need to be alone."

"Will you at least talk to Rachel?" asked Drew.

"Later."

"You going to be okay?" asked Dave.

I just nodded. I got up from my behind my desk.

"I'm going for a run," I announced as I walked out of my office.

I walked down the hall to the suite. I changed into a set of my running clothes that I kept in the closet. I laced up my running shoes and headed toward Central Park.

I ran hard and a I ran fast. I followed my usual path. But it wasn't my usual time. I thought about Rachel as I passed the spot of our first sexual encounter.

What was I going to do about Rachel? I didn't know how I could handle the news I had just received about Matt and continue to work through my commitment issues. It was possible that I loved Rachel. Was that enough for me?

CHAPTER 49

Rachel

Justin texted me. He had just finished a run and wanted to talk. I knew something was wrong. Justin never ran at this time of day. Also, his message was rather cryptic and concerned me.

I met him at a coffee shop around the corner from *Renaud's*. He was freshly showered and wearing a pair of jeans and a New York Giants sweatshirt. Strange outfit as the restaurant would be opening for dinner soon. Another sign something was wrong.

"What's wrong?" I asked as soon as he sat down at the table.

Justin told me that Matt was behind the stolen money at the restaurant. He also told me that Matt had been involved in money laundering at the hotel that he had managed and that Nick had been part of it. Apparently, Matt placed Nick at *Renaud's* to switch the money laundering operation from the hotel to the restaurant.

"Oh my gosh," I said. "Justin, I am so sorry. That is simply awful. But what doesn't make sense is why they were stealing. I'm no expert, but isn't money laundering running criminal money through the books of a legitimate business? Or something like that?"

"Yeah. That was the plan. I though about that also while I was on my run. I called Drew and Dave. They explained that Matt and Nick owed somebody money that they needed to pay quick. Stealing a little at a time was to cover that. Matt figured they would replace the money before we noticed. His plan was to get a job helping me manage the restaurant and then he would set up the money laundering scheme."

We sat quietly for a few minutes. Neither one of us knew what to say. I couldn't believe that Matt was a criminal and what he was doing, and planned to do, at *Renaud's*. It explained Justin's behavior that afternoon.

"Rachel, I don't know how to say this," Justin said.

"I don't like the sound of that," I said.

"I think I need a little time."

"Are you breaking up with me?"

"No. I just need time to think. I'm taking a little time off from the restaurant and getting out of the city for a short vacation."

"I'll go with you. I have plenty of vacation time."

"No. I need to be alone. I need time sort some things out."

"About your brother?"

"Yes. And about how to trust other people."

"You don't trust me?"

"It's not that. Not directly. It's just . . . if my own brother can do what he did."

Justin looked away. He stared out the window on the busy New York street. He probably wondered how he could know and trust me any more than the strangers on the street. I could feel tears welling up in my eyes.

"I'm sorry, Rachel. Give me some time. I'll call you when I get back in a few weeks."

That was it. It was all Justin said to me. He got up and walked out of the coffee shop. I watched him walk away.

I was shocked and confused. Justin hadn't broken up with me, but he hadn't exactly made me feel good about where he was in our relationship. I began to cry as I felt Justin would find it easier to go back to not being committed to anyone. Maybe Matt took Justin's ability to trust away from him.

I got up from the table and caught a taxi home. I cried the entire ride home. I had to assure the taxi driver I was okay. I wasn't, but there was nothing he could do to help me.

I managed to sneak past Frank without him seeing my puffy red eyes. Megan was at dinner with Zack. I entered my empty apartment and kicked my shoes off at the door. I took a hot shower and then went to bed. I cried myself to sleep.

CHAPTER 50

Justin

"Where are you going?" asked Drew.

"I don't know. Aruba, Cancun, someplace tropical and warm," I said.

We sat at Drew's kitchen table. He attempted to bribe me with pizza and hot wings. I had taken two bites of my pizza and ate one chicken wing. I wasn't hungry.

"You can't just run a way from your problems," said Drew.

"What? Like dad?"

"It was a blessing when dad left. But, yeah, in a way he ran away. But he had run away from mom and us long before he moved out of the house."

"I'm not running away from anything," I said. "I just need a vacation. I need some time to think."

"Justin, I get it. I really do. This is hard on all of us. Shit, Matt is going to jail. He's a criminal. He lied to all of us. But don't mess up the rest of your life because of Matt's screw up."

"You mean with Rachel, don't you?"

"She's the best thing to ever happen to you, Justin. You know it. I know it. Everybody knows it. You are a different person, a better person, because of her."

"Don't you think I know that? But how can I really trust anyone after what Matt did? I don't know if I can ever trust anyone ever again."

"Including me?" asked Drew.

I paused for a moment. Drew had always been the one person in my life I could count on. He never let me down. He always looked out for me. If I couldn't trust Drew, I couldn't trust anyone.

"I didn't exactly meant it that way," I finally answered.

"But you're thinking if Matt can betray you . . ."

I shrugged my shoulders. I didn't want to admit it. Not then, not ever, but maybe I couldn't trust anyone. Not Rachel. Not Drew.

"Justin, do you love Rachel?"

"Tough question to answer."

"It only means you have thought about it."

I had thought about it. I thought about it a lot. I had even thought about inviting Rachel to go on vacation with me. But I quickly had put it out of my mind. Commitment and trust issues vetoed inviting her.

"Rachel is a first for me. At commitment. At a relationship. I don't know how the game is played," I finally said.

"Justin, it's not a game. What you were doing before? That may have been a game. Actually, I don't know what it was. I know it wasn't anything close to a relationship. It wasn't anything close to what you have with Rachel."

"Or had. I don't know if I can continue seeing her," I admitted.

It might have been a cry for help, so to speak. I knew if anyone could convince me to stay with Rachel, it would be Drew. *Is that what I wanted him to do?*

"Look, little bro, I know what Matt did stinks big time. I know it slammed us all hard in the chest. I still can't believe it myself. But you can't go through life detaching yourself from everyone you care about. Especially someone who you may be in love with."

"Are you sure you're a lawyer and not a therapist?"

"Well, I have spent most of my life looking out for you. I guess I've figured a few things out along the way."

I nodded and grinned. Then Drew and I sat for a while. Neither of us said anything. We didn't need to. Drew knew I would speak when I was ready.

"I don't want to lose her," I said softly.

"Then don't," Drew replied.

CHAPTER 51

Rachel

My phone range. It was Frank calling from the lobby.

"Hi, Frank."

"Rachel, Justin's here. Is it okay to send him up?"

"Yes. Thank you, Frank."

Ever since the incident with Roger the building policy had changed. The doormen always called residents before letting any non-resident into the building. A few moments later, there was a knock at my door.

I looked out the peephole just to be sure. I was also more cautious these days.

It was Justin. His amazing light brown eyes stared back at me. He was also holding flowers and a box of chocolates. I opened the door.

"I'm sorry. I was a fool. I didn't mean what I said at the coffee shop. Well, there is a lot I still need to figure out. But I don't want to figure them out without you."

"Come in," I said.

"These are for you," Justin said as he handed me the flowers and box of chocolates.

Even though Justin had taken great leaps forward in commitment, he still had never brought me flowers or chocolate. Until he showed up with both.

"I thought you didn't do flowers and chocolate?" I teased.

"I'm continuing to evolve," he said.

"Well, the flowers are lovely. And dark chocolate is my favorite. Good choice."

"Rachel, I love you."

I stopped in my tracks. My heart skipped a beat.

"I love you," he said again.

"I heard you the first time," I said.

"You're stunned. I know. But I mean it. I love you."

"I love you, too," I said. I put the flowers and candy on the table.

Justin took me into his arms and kissed me. It was the most intimate kiss we had ever shared. Justin had told me he loved me. His kiss left no doubt.

I knew we I could handle whatever life threw at us. We loved each other and it would carry us forward. He may have started out as Mr. Wrong, but it didn't matter. I knew I had found my Mr. Right.

Want more Sweet Romance?
Start reading *A Love That Will Last*
(turn the page for a preview)

Visit my website for a complete list of my books,
www.elliejadamsauthor.com

Preview of A Love That Will Last

Chapter 1
Taylor Madison

"You're what?" I asked. I'm sure the shock and confusion was very evident on my face.

"I'm sorry, Taylor. I just thought it would be better to do this before we left for winter break," said my boyfriend Jared. Now ex-boyfriend. As of thirty seconds ago, when he told me that he was breaking up with me.

I sat down on my bed in the dorm room that I shared with my best friend Stephanie. I felt so stupid. I thought Jared was coming by to exchange our Christmas presents and to fool around before the month-long break. Tears began to well up in my eyes.

"Please, Taylor, don't cry. You know I can't handle you crying."

"You should have thought of that before you decided to break up with me so abruptly," I sobbed.

"I didn't just decide to do this. I've been trying to get up the nerve to tell you for a few weeks."

"Gee, that makes me feel a lot better."

"Taylor, you are great . . ."

"Don't even think of giving me the it's not you, it's me line. Okay? That won't make this any easier."

"Okay. I won't."

"Is there someone else?" I asked through my tears.

"No. Not one girl, anyway. I just want to be able to see other people. We have dated for two years. Two good years, but I don't want to get tied down this young."

"Oh, so now I am the old ball and chain?"

"I didn't say that." Jared sat on the end of my bed. "Taylor, it's scary how much I like you. But I'm only twenty-one. You are the only girl that I have really dated."

"Just not your forever," I said.

"I should go. I have to catch the shuttle to the airport." Jared stood and started to cross the room toward the door. He paused for a moment at the door. "Goodbye, Taylor." He opened the door and walked out. The door closed gently behind him.

I flopped over onto my side and crawled up in the fetal position and balled my eyes out. I had mostly cried myself dry when Stephanie came into the room.

"Taylor, what's wrong?" She asked as she rushed toward my bed. I sat up, clutching facial tissues in my hand.

"Jared broke up with me."

"What? When? No, it doesn't matter. . . . what a jerk! He doesn't deserve you." Stephanie was going through the list of all the things your best friend should say when your boyfriend dumps you. She put her arm around me and held me close as she did.

"I didn't see it coming. I had no idea. I must be really stupid."

"Taylor Madison, you are far from stupid. Jared Hunter is the stupid one. How on earth could he let you go. He will never find anyone as good as you. Ever."

"Apparently, he doesn't think that." I wiped my eyes and blew my nose. Stephanie grabbed the trash can and held it out so that I could throw the used tissues in. Then she placed it on the floor next to my feet for the deposit of more used tissues to come.

"I know that you don't want to hear this right now, but there will be someone else. Lots of fish in the sea. I passed at least a half dozen very eligible guys on my way back to the dorms."

"I know you're right. I just don't think I am ready to hear it right now. But I appreciate the sentiment."

"Did he give you a reason?" Stephanie asked.

"Kinda, sorta. . . . He wants to date other girls. Have more experiences. He said that he is too young to be getting really serious with one person."

"He should have thought of that two years ago."

"Maybe he's right. I'm not even twenty-one . . ."

"Just six more weeks," interjected Stephanie. "Then you are a legal beagle all the way."

"You know, I was so looking forward to coming back and celebrating my 21st birthday. I was imagining what special thing that Jared might be planning to surprise me."

"Taylor, I know that it hurts. This truly, truly, stinks. But you can't start dwelling on stuff like that. It will only make you crazy. You know what?"

"What?"

"We have an entire winter break to help you forget all about Jared."

"I don't want to forget him. We had a good relationship. Until forty-five minutes ago. And it's not like he cheated on me or something."

"Not that you know of."

"Stephanie."

"You're right. Sorry. Jared is uber stupid for letting you go, but he is not a cheater."

I nodded my head.

"Okay, so let's ditch the idea of making you forget Jared. But we still need to help you move on. But let's be sure to pack an extra box of tissues for the car," said Stephanie.

There was a knock at our door. Stephanie padded over and answered.

"You girls need any help packing your car?" It was our friend Cody. I loved him like a brother, but this was definitely the wrong time for him to stop by. He's had a huge crush on me since freshman orientation. I just couldn't deal with him at the moment.

Despite her attempt to convince me that I should hook up with some random guy, Stephanie knew exactly what I was thinking most of the time. And she always stepped up for me when it counted. "Nope. I think we are good," she said peeking her head out the door. "Thanks for checking, though. Have a great break. See you the end of January."

Stephanie closed the door. "Was that too harsh?"

"A little abrupt," I replied.

"Do you want me to get him back?"

"No. That is okay. Cody will be fine." And that is the truth. Cody was like Teflon.

I also had what I needed at the moment. A hug from my best friend.

Stephanie Moore and I have been best friends since her family moved in next door to my family the summer before third grade. We have shared pretty much all of life's experiences together. Including a dream to attend Stanford University. So we were over the moon when we both got accepted. I'm majoring in Human Resources Management and Stephanie is majoring in boys and English Literature. In that order.

Where I can be serious. Stephanie is silly. I am also the more level headed of the two of us. A fact that Stephanie will freely admit. We compliment each other in nearly every aspect of our lives. I love her like a sister and couldn't imagine life without her. We would do anything for each other.

"Thanks for being my friend," I said to her.

"Are you kidding? Just try to get rid of me."

I smiled. I was still sick over Jared breaking up with me, but it was a small step in the right direction. Just having Stephanie with me made it a little better. She could be a real firecracker, but she had a heart of gold and was loyal as the day is long. She is also one of the prettiest girls that I know. But she would also say that about me.

Frankly, Stephanie is closer to the gorgeous end of the spectrum. I am more on the average pretty end. Stephanie is 5'6" tall, slender, and has stunning curves that truly fill out a dress. I think she also has the most perfectly proportioned face. Her long dark hair is full-bodied and has a wonderful sheen. Her chestnut eyes are warm and also sparkle with a hint of her playfulness.

I am 5'5" tall and my weight is proportionate to my height. I have long dirty blonde hair and electric blue eyes. I guess you would say that I have a cute figure.

"What are you thinking?" Stephanie asked me.

"Do you remember Bobby Wheeler?"

"Yeah. He was kind of a dork."

"That's him," I replied with a chuckle. "I was just thinking about past boyfriends."

"We're not going to start feeling bad about ourselves? Are we?" asked Stephanie.

"No worse than I already feel about being dumped by Jared."

"I guess I'll take that. For now. But the goal is to start feeling better."

I glanced at the clock. "We should probably finish packing. We have a pretty long drive ahead of us," I said.

"Road trip, baby!"

Stephanie always got excited to travel the 358 miles between school and home. I saw it as five hours and forty-five minutes in a car. I didn't like to be in a car more than two hours. Stephanie tried to make the trips as fun as possible. She programmed special road trip jams into her iPod and packed plenty of snacks. We also stopped every two hours for a bathroom break and to stretch our legs.

I was looking forward to getting home for our holiday break. Especially now. There is nothing like my mom's home cooked meals and sleeping in my own bed. But this trip would change me in ways that I least expected.

Chapter 2

"I could have helped you with that," said Cody from behind us. Stephanie and I had just put our suitcases in the trunk of my car. I closed the trunk and whirled around.

If it had been anyone other than Cody, there would be serious personal space violations going on at the moment. He was a close friend and it was part of what made Cody, Cody. He's like a puppy. Easily excitable, doesn't know any better, can be annoying at times, but adorable and harmless.

"We're good. Thanks, Cody," I said. Stephanie went and got in the passenger's side of the car. A subtle hint that we were ready to leave. Cody didn't pick up on subtle hints. He was just staring adoringly at me with his puppy dog eyes.

"Your eyes are red and a little puffy," he noted. "Have you been crying?"

"Allergies," I said. I didn't want to get into a conversation about Jared dumping me. I really did just want to get in my car and head home for the holidays. Cody wrinkled his nose.

"You don't have allergies this time of year," he stated. Cody knew almost as much about me as Stephanie. Not that I shared all that much with him. But he had two and half years of close observation. I'd be creeped out if it weren't Cody. But, again, he is completely harmless. He maintains his fantasy that we will one day end up together, but he is also a nice friend.

"Must be something in the air today. I don't know."

"Well, you can develop new allergies. But it would make more sense if it were springtime. Lots of pollen in the air then. Probably not that. Did you try a new perfume?" He sniffed like a bloodhound. He shook his head as negative on the new perfume. "Did you have something different to eat today?"

"No. My usual breakfast. Nothing out of the ordinary for lunch." *Come on* , Taylor. What is wrong with you? I should have just said "Yes. That must be it." and then excused myself.

"Hmm. Very peculiar," said Cody.

"I'm sure whatever it is will be fine in a little while. It's already better. When are you leaving for break?"

"Tonight. My parents are coming to pick me up after work. I really need to get my own car. It is such a bummer needing my parents to drop me off and pick me up all the time."

Stephanie gave two short blasts of the car horn.

"Stephanie is anxious to get on the road. We have a long drive ahead of us. Have a nice break, Cody."

"Oh, yeah. Right. Okay. You have a nice break too. I'll call you."

"Okay. See you next month." I walked to the driver's side door and got in. I put on my seat belt and started the car. I put the shift in drive and we eased forward. I saw Cody in the rear view mirror as he watched us drive away.

Stephanie laughed. "He is one of a kind," she said.

"That he is. But he is sweet. And adorable in his way."

"Sort of like a lost puppy," said Stephanie.

"I was just thinking that," I said.

We exited Stanford's campus and worked our way to I-280. We then took CA-85 and US-101 South to CA-152 East. We'd follow CA-152 to I-5 South. I-5 would take us into Los Angeles. We knew the route by heart. Both ways.

"The Jetta runs much better than your old car," Stephanie commented.

"I know. I love it."

Last summer I had saved up enough money to buy a used 2008 Volkswagen Jetta. It had over 80,000 miles on it, but was in great condition. But I was sold on its metallic blue color. It ran great. I was very happy with what was still a relatively "new" car to me. Since we went pretty much everywhere together, and Stephanie didn't have her own car, she chipped in for the insurance, maintenance, and gas. It worked out well for both of us.

"Okay. Time for road jams part one," Stephanie announced. She plugged her iPod in and soon we were singing along to Maroon 5's Move's Like Jagger. I gave it no more than two Maroon 5 songs before Stephanie would comment about Adam Levine. He is, without a doubt, her top celebrity crush. She only lasted the one song.

"You do know that Adam Levine and Maroon 5 are from Los Angeles?" she said.

"I think everybody who knows Maroon 5 knows that."

"Just sayin'."

"What? That because both you and Adam Levine are from LA that you might meet one day?"

"Could happen."

"He's married now."

"I know. It would still be very cool to meet him. We should try to get tickets to be in the audience for The Voice."

"We're at school during the shows."

"I'm sure we could find time to get to one of the shows."

"Okay. You figure that out."

"Don't be so dismissive of the idea," said Stephanie.

"You're right. I'm sorry. If we can make the schedule work, we can definitely try to get tickets."

"All I'm asking."

We sang our way through the first part of our road trip jams. We made our first stop of the trip at the two hour mark. More songs, more girl talk, and a break at our four hour mark. As we got back in the car, we set off for the last leg of our tip. If traffic cooperated, we would be home in under two hours. It did, and one hour and forty-three minutes later we pulled into my driveway. We were greeted by my sister Victoria, a senior in high school, and my little brother, Daniel, who was in sixth grade. We hugged them both.

"Mom and Dad want us to meet them and the Moore's at Maria's for dinner. They are all heading there after work," said Victoria. Maria's was a favorite Italian restaurant of both our families. We had many joint family dinners there.

"Mom said she promises to make your favorite dinner tomorrow night," added Daniel.

"Yay," I cheered. My favorite meal was my mom's baked macaroni and cheese. Nothing fancy. Just great comfort food. "Have you grown since Thanksgiving?" I asked Daniel.

"An inch and a quarter," he proudly replied.

Daniel was on the smaller size for his age. Literally every inch he grew was a big deal in our house. We were all waiting for a growth spurt that his doctor said would come. It couldn't come soon enough. Poor Daniel was being bullied at school because of his size.

"Okay, big guy," I said, "why don't you help me get my luggage in the house."

"You got it," he said.

"Meet up in five minutes to leave for Maria's?" I said to Stephanie.

"You got it," she said and she winked at Daniel. My little brother had a crush on Stephanie. This was a fairly recent development. Up until a year or so ago, girls were still icky. That had all changed.

"See ya in a few," Daniel said to Stephanie.

We put my suitcase in my bedroom. I went to the bathroom and washed up for dinner. We met Stephanie back at my car in the driveway. We piled into my Jetta and headed for Maria's. Fifteen minutes later we were circling Maria's parking lot for a place to park.

I looked in the rear view mirror at Victoria and Daniel in the backseat. "Why don't we drop you two off and we'll circle around again for a parking space. Just let Mom and Dad know we are parking the car."

They both shrugged their shoulders and gave me the universal teenage whatever look. I stopped in front of the entrance to Maria's and Victoria and Daniel got out.

"Maybe we should try around back," suggested Stephanie.

"Good idea. Probably more parking back there."

I looped the car around the restaurant and headed into the back parking lot.

"There's a spot." Stephanie pointed to a spot on the end of the next row.

"Probably the best we are going to get this time of night," I said. I pulled into the spot and turned off the engine.

Just as Stephanie and I were getting out of the car, a sports car raced around the corner and careened into the back corner of the Jetta.

Chapter 3

"What the heck?!" Stephanie blurted out. We both thought it. She said it.

"You okay?" I asked.

"Yeah. You?"

"I'm fine. I don't know about the back of my car, though."

We both got out.

"Oh, I am so sorry. Are you two okay?" Asked the driver of the sports car.

I almost forgot about the smashed rear end of my car. I was looking at one of the most handsome guys that I had ever seen. Handsome, but in a stay away from him, sort of way. And not just because he had hit my car.

The tall stranger was lean, but athletic. He had a handsom oval face with full, pink, lips, and a perfectly proportioned nose. His steel blue eyes carried both danger and allure. He ran his long fingers through his spiky, dirty blond hair. He looked to be about my age. He was wearing faded jeans, a plain black t-shirt, and well-worn tennis sneakers. But the car he was driving was worth a lot more than a used car with over 80,000 miles on it.

"Where the heck did you learn to drive, jerkface?!" Stephanie screamed.

"I said I was sorry. I'll pay for the damage."

"You bet you will," said Stephanie. "You can certainly afford it."

The guy bent down and looked at the damage. He was really cute. "Tail light is busted and the rear bumper is cracked. Other than that, I don't think there is any more damage."

"We'll let the police and an insurance adjuster decide just how much damage there is," said Stephanie. I think she honestly forgot that I was even standing there. She does have a bit of a take charge personality.

"Look, no need to get the police involved. Or our insurance companies. I can pay you right now for the damage. Cash. And more than enough to cover the repairs."

"Hold the phone there, Richie Rich. –"

"Please," he pleaded. "One more mark on my driving record and I could loose my license. Plus, my dad will take my car away from me."

I should have been upset with him for hitting my car. But I was feeling entirely something else. This guy had a hard outer shell, but he certainly knew being vulnerable. He had layers. I was instantly hit with a desire to peel back those layers.

His eyes flashed on me. They were an intriguing mystery. Both cool and distant. Telling me to stay away. And, at the same time, there was a warmth behind them. Captivating and inviting.

Stephanie felt none of what I was feeling. "Oh, boo hoo rich boy. You won't have your fancy sports car to drive around LA and cause damage to other people's property," she said.

"Wait a second, Stephanie," I said. "The damage really isn't that bad. If, ah . . ."

"Kyle."

"If Kyle wants to pay for the damage, I don't have a problem with that."

"What? Who are you, and what have you done with my best friend? You are usually the responsible one," Stephanie said to me. "Isn't this why we have insurance?"

"Yes, but –"

"But, what? I'm sure if Kyle here can afford a Ferrari, he can afford car insurance. We're supposed to call the police and the insurance company when there is an accident."

Stephanie was absolutely correct. But I didn't care. I wasn't concerned with going strictly by the book on this one. I felt strangely bad for Kyle.

"It's a minor fender bender. Barely that."

"So this is your car? Not her's?" asked Kyle.

"Yes. Although she helps pay for upkeep, gas, and insurance," I said.

"Right. Insurance that we purchase in case there is an accident." Stephanie added with a huff.

"Can you excuse us for a moment?" I said to Kyle. I took Stephanie by the arm and walked a few steps away.

"Look, you are one hundred percent right about what we should do," I said in a hushed tone. "I am not disagreeing with you on that. But it was an accident. He apologized and is being super nice about this. Let's give the guy a break and let him pay for the damage."

"Oh, I get it," Stephanie responded in an equally hushed tone, "you like this guy."

"No I don't. That's crazy. Don't be ridiculous. I just –"

"You just nothing. You like him."

"I'll admit that he is cute." I shifted my eyes and glanced over at Kyle. "Disturbingly handsome, actually. But, I do not like him. I don't even know him. All I am saying is that he seems nice and wants to pay for the damage. Where's the harm in that?"

"He's trouble, Taylor. T-R-O-U-B-L-E."

"I'm not looking for a date. I just want him to pay for the damage so we can go have dinner with our families."

"Fine. Whatever. It's your car. Just make sure that he gives you enough for the repairs. And not some cheap repair job, either. A good garage."

"Okay. Sounds like a plan."

"And let the record show that I don't agree with your decision. And let it further show that I am right about what should be happening."

"Duly noted," I said. I looked up and over at Kyle. He was leaning against his car like he didn't have a care in the world. I think he already knew which way this was going. He seemed like he read most situations before other people did.

Stephanie and I stepped back toward the cars. "Okay," I said. "I'll let you pay for the damage."

"Great. Much easier this way."

"For you," Stephanie huffed.

"For all of us," I said as I glanced at Stephanie.

Kyle pulled a large roll of cash out of his pocket. He peeled of a number of $100 bills and handed them to me. Certainly more than enough to get my car fixed.

His hand lightly brushed against mine as he handed me the money. I melted inside. Jared, who? Okay, it wasn't quite that dramatic. I was still upset at Jared breaking up with me. But the sensation caused by Kyle's skin touching mine was completely unexpected. I felt like a giddy little girl.

Kyle's voice filtered through my haze. "Let me pay for your dinner tonight as well. You know, for your trouble."

"Um, well, I don't know. No. I mean, that is nice of you, but you've paid for the damage to my car. That is enough."

"What?!" interjected Stephanie. "If he wants to pay for our dinner, let him."

"Listen to your friend. I'd really like to cover your dinner. I feel really bad about the trouble I've caused you."

"But we are having dinner with our families . . ."

"No problem. Whatever the cost of dinner. In fact, order the best meals. It's the least that I can do."

"Darn straight," said Stephanie. "Taylor, you are saving Kyle here from a world of hurt with the DMV and his mommy and daddy. Besides, its not like he can't afford it."

"There's no need to be rude, Stephanie," I said.

Kyle looked at me and smiled. A smile that knocked me off guard.

"Taylor, huh? Like Taylor Swift." Kyle said to me.

I felt myself blushing. "Um, yeah. She's a bit older than me, though. I guess it was still a popular name the year I was born, too. Or, I guess, my parents just liked the name. I don't know. I've never really asked them." I ramble when I get nervous.

"However you got your name. I like it. It suits you," he said.

"Thanks. Kyle's a nice name too." Seriously? Is that the best you can come up with? I felt really stupid.

"We really need to get inside for dinner with our families," Stephanie said.

"Just tell the waiter or waitress to send me the bill. Kyle Bennett. They all know me in Maria's," said Kyle.

"Okay. Thanks, Kyle."

"Sure thing, Taylor. And, again, I'm sorry about your car."

"No problem. I've got the cash to get it fixed," I said as I patted my pocket where I had put the stack of hundred dollar bills.

Stephanie tugged at my arm and pulled me toward the restaurant.

"You were a little rude to him," I said.

"And you were too nice. You stay as far away as possible from guys like Kyle."

"He didn't seem so bad to me. Besides, I thought you said I needed someone to help me get over breaking up with Jared."

"Yes. But not Kyle."

"Why not Kyle?"

"Trust me. I know the type. He's not a guy that you are ready to handle. In fact, he's not a guy that you would ever be ready to handle. I wouldn't even hook up with a guy like him."

"You make him sound so dangerous," I said.

"In a way, he is. Trust me on this, Taylor. Forget about Kyle."

Stephanie knew a lot more about guys than I did. I will give her that. And I'm confident that she is right about Kyle. But for a few moments I had forgotten about being dumped by my boyfriend of two years. Maybe it was worth having my tail light smashed.

In the end, I knew that Stephanie was probably right. I chalked my meeting Kyle up to a brief escape. Back to reality. Besides, it wasn't like I was ever going to see Kyle Bennett again.

Chapter 4

Maria's Restaurant was a modern Italian restaurant. The main entrance is bright and warm with light toned bamboo wood floors, sage colored walls, and a marble host station. A tall, sleek, glass vase stood behind the host desk with a full and colorful flower arrangement.

We waited a moment as the host helped the couple in front of us. To the right was a small sitting area with a beige leather sofa and armchairs. They were against a wall that was set with horizontally laid long, flat, brick.

Beyond the seating area was the bar. There were bar chairs that matched the leather of the seating area. The bar itself had a light yellow front and a dark granite top. There were several, highly polished, light wood round tables. They sat either two or up to five with high-backed chairs with the same beige leather.

"Fancy meeting you here." I heard Kyle's voice behind us.

I turned and looked up into his steel blue eyes. They caught the light from above us and had a bluish-gray sparkle. Again I saw both danger and allure in them.

"Um, uh, we are just waiting to be seated with our families." I stammered. Darn how I ramble when I am nervous. But why am I nervous? Danger and allure, that's why.

"Have you eaten here before?" Kyle asked me.

"Lots of times. Our families love it here," I said trying to sound cool and collected.

Kyle nodded his head in agreement. "I think they have the best lasagna around. But I don't get here very often."

"Family or friend?" I asked.

"Excuse me?"

"For dinner, I mean. Are you meeting a family member or friend for dinner? Or maybe a date?"

"Oh. Of course. A friend . . . of sorts."

Odd reply, I thought.

"Welcome to Maria's. May I help you?" The host asked.

"We're up," said Stephanie. She had ignored Kyle and hadn't even bothered to turn around.

"Excuse me," I said to Kyle.

"Enjoy your dinner. Remember, have them send the check to me. Kyle Bennett."

I nodded my understanding as Stephanie gave a slight tug on my arm. "Yes, we are with the Madison and Moore party," Stephanie informed the host.

"Right this way," the host replied.

I watched as Kyle walked through the sitting area and into the bar. He headed toward a table for two and sat down opposite a stunningly gorgeous young woman. A friend, of sorts.

"Taylor. You coming?" Stephanie called to me. I turned and followed her. The main dining room had the same light yellow walls as on the front of the bar. Various works of art hung on the walls around the dining room.

The room was pretty big and was furnished with the highly polished light wood tables and high-backed leather chairs. The dining room tables sat anywhere from two to eight. Most sat four or five.

We were at a table for eight. Just enough to accommodate both our families. Our parents stood as we approached. My parents hugged me. Stephanie's parents hugged her. Then we traded hugs with each others' parents.

"You both look wonderful," said my mom.

"How was the drive down from Stanford?" asked Stephanie's mom.

"Fine," I said.

"Until we reached the parking lot," added Stephanie.

"Why? What happened?" asked my dad.

Stephanie and I both sat. Stephanie was to my right. Victoria was to my left. Next to Vicki was Daniel, and then my mom, and my dad. Next to my dad was Stephanie's dad, then her mom. Stephanie was an only child. But Vicki and Daniel were like siblings to her.

"Oh, it was nothing. Just a little fender bender," I said.

"Are you both alright?" asked both our moms at the same time.

"We're fine," I said.

"Yeah, we're fine. Taylor's got a busted tail light and cracked bumper," said Stephanie.

My dad said, "But you filed a police report and called the insurance company?"

Stephanie flashed her eyes my way, but stayed silent.

"Taylor? You did contact the police and insurance company, right?" my dad asked.

"There was no need to," I replied. "The damage was minimal. The guy who hit us paid me in cash to cover the repairs."

My dad said, "Taylor. What have we always told you? . . ."

"I know. I know. But, really, Dad, the damage is not that bad. Kyle gave me more than enough money to cover the repairs. He's also paying for our dinner."

"Kyle?" my mom asked.

"Kyle is the guy's name. Kyle Bennett."

"So he just gave you cash?" asked my mom.

"Yes. See?" I pulled the wad of hundred dollar bills out of my pocket.

"That looks like a lot of money," said my mom. "Who walks around with that much cash?"

"Rich dudes," Stephanie said.

"And drug dealers," said Stephanie's mom.

"Mom, you watch too many crime shows," Stephanie replied.

"Mrs. Moore, I don't think he is a drug dealer," I said.

"I agree with Taylor. Probably not a drug dealer. Just a spoiled rich guy. You should have seen the car he was driving."

"Yeah? What kind of car?" asked Stephanie's dad. He was a real car aficionado.

"I don't know. Some sort of Ferrari. I recognized the logo on the car," Stephanie answered.

"Keep dreaming," Mrs. Moore teased her husband.

"Let me see that cash," my dad said to me. I handed him the money. He flipped through the bills discretely. He selected one randomly and examined it closely. "Certainly looks real," he announced.

"What? Were you thinking the money was fake?" I asked.

"Doesn't hurt to be sure," he replied. He put the cash into his pocket. "Tomorrow we will go to Hank's Garage. He does good work and will give you a fair price. Next time, though, young lady –"

" I know. Call the police and the insurance company," I said.

Stephanie gave me a look of pure satisfaction. I pretended like I didn't notice. We both knew that I had. She gave me a playful nudge with her left elbow. I flashed her quick grin.

"Well, let's hope there never is a next time," said my mom.

"True," said Stephanie's mom.

"So, is this Kyle fellow really picking up the check for dinner?" my dad asked.

"He said he would. I don't have any reason to doubt him," I replied.

"Well, if the cash and the car are any indication, neither do I," said my dad.

"He also told us to order whatever we wanted. To get the best bottle of wine," I said.

"Oh, I don't think we should take advantage like that," said my mom. We were so much a like, it could be scary sometimes.

"I told him that it wasn't necessary. You know, to pay for dinner. And certainly not to treat us to the most expensive bottle of wine. But, he insisted," I said.

"I guess your mother is right," my dad said. "We'll order what we would normally order and nothing more. Nonetheless, I think we should accept Mr. Bennett's offer to pay for dinner. The least he can do for avoiding points on his insurance," said my dad.

"Scott, do really think we should let him pay for our dinner?" asked my mom.

"Sure. Why not? It is a nice gesture that he made. And if Taylor says that he insisted –"

"He did, actually. Twice." I said.

"What do you think Rachel? John?" my mother asked the Moore's.

"I don't see the harm in it. He probably feels very bad about the accident and appreciative that Taylor accepted the cash for the repairs rather than filing a report," said John Moore.

"I think, under the circumstances, it would be okay," agreed Stephanie's mom.

"Yeah," said Stephanie, "he was all worried about losing his driver's license or having his parents taking his car away from him."

"How old is this Mr. Bennett?" asked Stephanie's dad.

"About our age, I would guess," answered Stephanie.

"Well, I think this will be a good lesson for the young man," said my dad.

"Well, if he is as rich as the girls say, I'm not sure how much of a lesson he will learn from this. I mean, the cost of the repairs and dinner is probably nothing to him," said my mom.

"Well, I think that confirms it," said my dad. "Let's order."

After we ordered dinner, our parents asked us how our final exams went and what we were taking for courses during the spring semester. Then we talked about our plans for winter break. Both Stephanie and I were hoping to pick up some hours at the grocery store that we had worked at over the past four summers. We usually picked up several hours a week over break.

"Do you plan on working there next summer as well?" my dad asked. "Final summer before graduation. Wow, that is hard to believe. You two will be college seniors next year. Where does the time go?"

"Actually, I was thinking of applying for an internship next summer," I said.

"Really? Where?" asked my dad.

"Human Resources Management at Bennworth Corporation."

"That sounds promising," said my dad. "They are a large company. It can help you get your foot in the door."

"Exactly what I am thinking," I said. "Bennworth is known for hiring from their internship pool. In fact, those who make good impressions during their internships are almost guaranteed a job offer."

"When would you need to apply, dear?" my mother asked me.

"No later than March first. I've already talked to my professors about writing recommendations. I'll probably start working on my essay over break."

"And when do they make their decision?" asked my dad.

"I think the end of April," I replied.

"Still gives you time to arrange for a summer position if it doesn't work out," said my dad.

"Don't be silly, Scott, Taylor is going to get the internship," said my mom.

"Thanks, Mom," I said. "But Dad is right. It is highly competitive."

"They would be crazy not to accept you for the internship. Where are they going to find a better Human Resources Management major than you?"

My mom thought that her children were the best at everything. She wasn't one of those moms that bragged to other moms, but she never held back on telling us how wonderful she knew we were. She may see things a bit through mommy rose colored glasses, but at least she was supportive.

My dad was equally supportive, but far more realistic and practical. That was one area where I tended to be more like my dad. That is probably why it surprised me so much that I even feigned the notion that I might even consider anything happening with Kyle Bennett. Assuming that he even would be interested in me. A major, unlikely, assumption. So, an assumption that I was not even making.

We finished our dinner and told the waiter that Kyle Bennett had offered to pick up the check. A few minutes later he returned and told us that we were all set. Kyle, obviously, made good on his offer to pay for dinner. I wasn't surprised. Despite Stephanie's protests, I didn't think that Kyle was such a bad guy.

As we left Maria's Restaurant, I wondered if Kyle was still having dinner with his "friend." I tried to peek as we passed the bar lounge, but didn't want to look obvious. I couldn't see beyond the groups of people, anyway. The seating area was more crowded than earlier. People sitting and standing with buzzers in their hands, waiting for a table to become available.

I followed the Moore's and my family out of the restaurant.

"Be careful driving home," said my dad. "Especially with a busted tail light. Other than taking the car to Hank's tomorrow, it stays in the driveway until it is fixed."

"Okay. See you at home," I replied. I was only half paying attention. I had got a glimpse of Kyle and the stunning young woman through the window. She was running her hand along his arm. They were talking and smiling. Stephanie caught me looking.

"Let it go, Taylor," she said. "See that girl he is with?"

"Of course. How can I not. She's gorgeous."

"That's not what I meant."

"What, then?"

"Guys like Kyle don't have girlfriends. They don't commit to relationships."

"How do you know? How do you know any of that is true?"

"Like I said, I know the type. Trust me. Come on, let's go."

I had a wet dream about Kyle that night. I'm not sure what sort of game my subconscious was playing on me. Maybe raw emotions. I was still getting over Jared breaking up with me. I hadn't even told my family yet.

When I woke I remembered the dream vividly. It had been about Kyle and I on a romantic date. But that's all that it was – a dream. I figured that was all it was ever going to be.

****

Start reading *A Love That Will Last*
Visit my website for a complete list of my books,
elliejadamsauthor.com

****

Would you like a free story?
Join my Newsletter and receive a Sweet Romance story as my gift to you. You will also receive author updates, new release

alerts, and exclusive contests and discounts. Free to Join. No Spam. Unsubscribe Anytime. Join at elliejadamsauthor.com

Newsletter

Join my Newsletter and receive a Sweet Romance story as my gift to you. You will also receive author updates, new release alerts, and exclusive contests and discounts. Free to Join. No Spam. Unsubscribe Anytime. Join at www.elliejadamsauthor.com

Books by Ellie J. Adams

For a complete list of my Sweet Romance books, visit:
www.elliejadamsauthor.com

About the Author

Ellie J. Adams's books have been downloaded over half-a-million times by readers around the world. She is a romantic at heart and likes her characters to find their Happily Ever After. Ellie's books offer moments of drama, humor, and heartache along the way. Her leading men are strong, but flawed, males, and the leading women are sweet, smart, and independent. Ellie writes sweet romance you can get swept up in and takes you away.